"What choice?" Fern said bitterly

She knew she was defeated, and her hatred of him was almost a physical pain.

"I'll go ahead with the arrangements, then," he said evenly, an expression of utter weariness crossing his face.

Fern had been so preoccupied with her own problems that she hadn't even considered how Piers must be feeling. He must be as reluctant as she was to enter into this cold-blooded union.

"I want this marriage, at least on the surface, to be conventional."

"You mean you'd prefer people not to know that you virtually blackmailed me into it," Fern said cuttingly. "You'd like me to play the part of the misty-eyed, ecstatic bride?"

"I'd settle for civility," he said mockingly.

ROSEMARY GIBSON was born in Cairo, where her father was in the Foreign Service. She spent her childhood in Egypt, Greece and Vietnam, returning to England at the age of eight. Though she took teacher's training at Christ Church College, her working experience has been varied— community-service worker, barmaid, gas-pump attendant, and ground hostess and receptionist for an airline in Bournemouth, where she first started writing seriously. She began with short stories for various women's magazines before becoming a romance novelist. She lives in New Forest with her dog, Cindy, and a black cat called Jellybean.

ROSEMARY GIBSON

to trust a stranger

Harlequin Books

TORONTO • NEW YORK • LONDON
AMSTERDAM • PARIS • SYDNEY • HAMBURG
STOCKHOLM • ATHENS • TOKYO • MILAN

Harlequin Presents first edition October 1991
ISBN 0-373-11403-6

Original hardcover edition published in 1990
by Mills & Boon Limited

TO TRUST A STRANGER

CHAPTER ONE

'THERE'S just this cheque for the farrier's and that's the lot.'
Fern Maynard placed an invoice in front of the fair-haired
man in his early thirties who sat behind the large oak desk.

David Warrender ignored the invoice, inscribed his name
with a flourish on the cheque and handed it back to the tall
girl with serious grey eyes, noting with approval the sensible
navy skirt and plain cream blouse, the businesslike way the
long nut-brown hair was coiled neatly into the base of her
neck.

'What would I do without my Miss Efficiency?'

'I dare say you'd survive,' Fern murmured lightly, and was
momentarily appalled by the underlying cynicism in her even
voice. She was aware, too, that the look of approval had
vanished from her employer's face, to be replaced by one of
minor irritation.

'Is anything the matter, Fern?'

She remained motionless for a second, her tranquil
expression giving no indication of the inner battle. Now,
she instructed herself forcefully. Tell him now. But she
delayed too long, as usual, running the carefully
rehearsed words through in her mind instead of uttering
them aloud. And the moment was lost as the fair man
rose to his feet, walked over to the latticed window and
stood gazing across the cobbled courtyard, shimmering
under the afternoon sun, and up to the large, imposing
red-bricked house beyond. His enquiry, Fern
acknowledged wryly, had been merely rhetorical
anyway; he hadn't expected or wanted an answer. Her

5

function, she had long ago accepted, was simply to ensure that life ran as smoothly and as agreeably as possible for David Warrender.

'Let's hope this weather holds until Saturday,' he murmured, turning to face her, and Fern's thoughts flew automatically to the impending Agricultural Show, an event held annually in the grounds of the Warrender estate. She had been hoping to take Carrie this year, but David had made it very evident this morning that he expected her to be at his beck and call all day Saturday. Other arrangements would have to be made for Carrie, she thought unhappily, envisaging the six-year-old's disappointment.

'You look so calm and cool, even in this unbearable heat.'

Fern forced her attention back to the fair man, conscious that he was now surveying her with a smile, the previous displeasure washed from his bland face. Then she stiffened as he took a step towards her, encircling her waist with his arms. She averted her face swiftly so that his lips missed her mouth and brushed the side of her cheek instead.

'For heaven's sake, what is the matter with you today, Fern?' he muttered querulously.

She lowered her eyes guiltily. 'It's so hot,' she murmured lamely, despising herself for the cowardice that had prompted the banal excuse.

'Damn it all, I'm not some over-amorous boss making a furtive pass at his secretary! We are supposed to be engaged——'

'Unofficially,' Fern broke in quickly, instantly regretting it, but at least the remark had the effect of making him release her from his suffocating embrace.

'Oh, so that's it.' His mouth curved down sulkily. 'I'm not allowed to touch until you're supporting the diamond ring. Or do I even have to wait until we're married?'

Fern's face tightened. 'David there's something——' she began quietly, but he interrupted her, hardly seeming to register that she had even been speaking.

'Darling, I'm so sorry. I didn't mean that.' His voice lowered and became wheedling. 'You know how I'd love to announce to the world that you've made me the happiest man alive, but I just want to give Mother a little more time to get to know you better first. She'll soon realise how perfect you are for me.'

Fern's face remained deadpan. She doubted whether Annette Warrender would ever condone the marriage between her beloved son and his mere secretary.

'Of course, I quite understand the situation,' she murmured steadily.

David shot her a quick glance, suspecting some hidden sarcasm, but decided that his reserved, self-contained Fern would be incapable of such malice. 'I knew you would.' He smiled, glancing at his gold wristwatch. 'I've arranged to meet Reg Parker at three to sort out the car parking for Saturday.' He paused in the doorway. 'See you tonight, darling. Around eight.'

Fern nodded and watched him depart from the office. She loathed the formal dinner parties which Annette Warrender hosted every few weeks and which David insisted that she attend. 'The more often she sees you, the quicker she'll come around.' Vividly she recalled David's words, and she knew that she ought to be laughing at the absurdity of a grown man needing his mother's approval in his choice of bride. She at the very least ought to be feeling indignant, if not downright furious at the implication that she was in some way inferior to David. Yet she didn't seem to feel anything, not even quiet amusement. Slowly, she walked out of the large room into the smaller outer office, her own domain, and moved across to the grey filing cabinet. Nothing seemed to touch her any more. Nothing seemed to matter much—except for Carrie. She had run the gauntlet of emotions, of anger, bitterness and despair long ago, and there was nothing left inside her, just numb lethargy.

She selected a file and then paused, staring out of the window up to the house. Crofters, the home of the Warrender family for generations. If she married David, she would one day be mistress of that daunting house.

She sighed and walked over to her desk, but found it impossible to concentrate on the open file in front of her. Sometimes she wondered if it was all a dream from which she would wake . . .

It had been two years ago when she'd answered an advertisement in the National Press for a secretary-cum-personal assistant to the owner of a country estate in the New Forest. The real attraction of the position had been the promise of a rent-free cottage on the estate for the successful candidate. She had been desperate to find a permanent home for herself and four-year-old Carrie.

She had been surprised and more than a little perturbed when David Warrender, her new employer and the most eligible bachelor in the district, had started to show more than a purely business interest in his twenty-four-year-old secretary. Warily, Fern had refused his invitations to dinner at first, only too conscious of the dangers of becoming personally involved with the man for whom she worked. He had persisted with his invitations and finally, driven by loneliness as much as anything else, she had accepted. She had enjoyed herself on that first occasion, Fern recalled ruefully, and had been reassured, when he made no attempt to touch her, that he wasn't looking for some brief, casual sexual liaison.

Fern stared down at her hands despondently. Why had she been so idiotic as to let things go so far? Not that David had actually proposed to her, simply seeming to take it for granted, when he announced his intention of marrying her, that she was certain to agree. And she had done nothing to dissuade him, Fern reminded herself guiltily, but simply continued with the pretence because it was easier, postponing the inevitable confrontation for as long as possible. Her eyes darkened, a wave of self-disgust swamping her as she relived those few days of weakness when she had been actually been tempted to go through with marrying David, forcing herself to view the whole situation coldly and clinically. Marriage to David Warrender represented security, a home for Carrie, freedom from all financial worries. That she wasn't in love with him, she had reasoned, would surely be an advantage. Never again did she want to feel that sensation of being totally out of control of a situation, be subjected to that irrational, destroying madness she'd once believed to be love. With David she would suffer no disillusionment, no anguish . . . but she couldn't marry him. She couldn't trade herself, not even for the sake of Carrie's future. It would be alien to her every instinct and totally unfair to David. And neither, she admitted, could she go on delaying telling him the truth—she must find an opportunity that evening to do so. Her expression tightened as she viewed the likely consequences of her action. Would David want her to go on working for him? She sighed. She couldn't face all that again, trying to find rented accommodation she could afford on a secretary's wages, minders for Carrie . . .

With a start, she stretched out a hand to the telephone, wondering how long it had been ringing while she'd been sitting there in a trance.

David hadn't returned to the office by five o'clock, so Fern carefully closed the office windows and locked the outer door with her own key. The heat was stifling as she stepped outside, and, squinting against the glare of the still powerful sun, she walked around the side of the converted stable block that was used as the estate office, and on to the footpath that led through Hollow Field and down to the River Avon. Normally, she drove back to Thyme Cottage after work, taking the most direct route down the lane, time being a precious commodity. But this evening there was no such urgency, no Carrie to collect from Mrs Jones in the village. Today, she was free to please herself.

Fern sauntered along the riverbank, the breeze from the water cooling on her face, consciously freeing her mind from all troublesome thoughts, determined to enjoy these few moments of solitude, a solitude that was all the more precious because it was a voluntary choice, and not, as so often in the past, a state enforced upon her.

The Avon slowed down, meandering under overhanging trees and widening to form a small, secluded pool. Ladies' Pool. The name had always intrigued Fern, conjuring up as it did a vision of young girls in bygone days, tripping down to the pool in their burdensome clothes to bathe in secret, away from prying eyes.

Swiftly, Fern stretched up a hand to her hair and released it from its confines, allowing it to cascade down her back in rich brown waves. She slipped off her shoes and sat down on the bank, dangling her legs over the edge, staring into the green water. No one came here to bathe any more. The heated pool at Crofters was far more enticing than this cool, deserted glade—except to her. She loved it here; her own small, private world.

Temptation proved to be too strong. Jumping to her feet, she discarded her skirt and blouse and dived headlong into the river, the icy contact on her heated skin making her laugh out loud with delighted shock. She swam round vigorously until she had warmed up and then rolled over on to her back, gazing up at the azure, cloudless sky, only just visible through the green canopy above. Perfect tranquillity. She had an insane urge to giggle, envisaging the staid expression on David's face if he could see her now, floating aimlessly in the water, clad only in her brief underwear. She was convinced that he would deem it unseeming behaviour in his secretary, let alone the future Mrs Warrender! The smile faded from her lips as she recalled her reaction when he had tried to kiss her earlier. Regardless of whether she wanted to marry David or not, surely she shouldn't feel quite such an aversion to a man as attractive as him? The physical aspect of their relationship was something else she had deliberately chosen to ignore over the past months, grateful rather than surprised that David made so few demands of her, seemingly being content with the exchange of unsatisfactory, brief goodnight kisses. Fern sighed. It was time she faced the truth. It wasn't just David she shied away from; the thought of intimacy with any man was now abhorrent to her. Was she frigid? she wondered drearily. Was that simply one more penalty she had to pay for the past?

Not wanting to pursue that painful line of thought, she executed a neat somersault and began to swim strongly under the water, revelling in the physical exertion that swept everything else from her mind.

The realisation that someone had grasped hold of her

shoulders and was pulling her up through the water came as a terrifying shock. She flailed her arms wildly, but before she had a chance to glimpse her attacker she was swung over on to her back and was being towed towards the bank.

'Let me go!' she yelped frantically and gulped a mouthful of water. Her desperate efforts to free herself were useless; she was imprisoned by arms that might just as well have been fashioned from steel.

'Don't panic. You're quite safe,' a deep male voice assured her calmly. Unceremoniously, she was lifted from the water and put on dry land.

'Are you out of your mind?' Fern's voice shook with incredulity as much as with outrage as she faced the man standing nonchalantly in front of her, arms folded indolently across his bare, tanned chest. His tousled dark hair glistened with water, and sodden Levis clung to powerful thighs and long, lean legs.

'Is that all the thanks I get for saving you from a watery grave?' he drawled, cool confident, blue eyes resting on her flushed face. 'And there was I expecting some token of your eternal gratitude.'

'You're crazy,' Fern stated flatly. 'I was in no more danger of drowning than of . . . flying to Mars,' she snapped. 'If you're that desperate to become a life-guard, try Bournemouth beach.' Her eyes narrowed. Had he genuinely thought she was in trouble? No, she dismissed the thought immediately. The man looked far too astute, far too assured to make such an error of judgement.

The blue eyes had moved from her face, lingering over her slim body, making her immediately conscious of her near-naked state. The wet, thin cotton bra and panties were virtually transparent—the expression in his eyes told her that.

'This is private property,' Fern said calmly, picking up

her clothes, ignoring the deep chuckle at her unintended *double entendre*. She slipped her skirt and blouse over her damp skin, deliberately not hurrying too obviously, determined that this man should not sense her acute embarrassment. Then, as she turned to face him again, she felt a twinge of fear for the first time, aware of just how secluded were her surroundings.

'I think you'd better leave,' she said, keeping her voice steady and devoid of any traces of panic. 'The owner dislikes trespassers on his land.'

'Really? You know the owner well?' the stranger enquired with interest, totally unperturbed.

'He happens to be my fiancé,' Fern replied haughtily, immediately wondering what had prompted her to admit that to this man of all people. Perhaps it had been simply through a desire to make him understand that she mattered to someone, someone who would take a very harsh view of his laying a hand on her. Unconsciously, she began to squeeze the water from her hair, pulling it back into its habitual severe style.

'Don't do that!'

Her stomach constricted as he took a silent step towards her, looming over her. She wanted to flee, there was something in his eyes that terrified her, but her legs wouldn't function properly. As if mesmerised, she felt strong hands curl into her hair, spreading it over her shoulders like a thick, soft velvet curtain.

'Beautiful,' he murmured softly, and then she felt his hand move under her chin, jerking it upwards so that she was forced to meet the compelling blue gaze.

She shut her eyes as if by doing that she could make him disappear, and then jolted as a firm, deft finger traced the outline of her compressed lips. Her eyes flickered open. His face was only a few inches away from her now; she could see the pulse beating at the base of the bronzed neck, feel the warmth of his breath on her skin. She stiffened, bracing herself for the inevitable, felt the hard mouth on hers and her mind fought, rebelling against the contact. Then she was only conscious of shock, the stunning realisation that the sensation wasn't distasteful, but was one of warm, drugging pleasure.

'Not too painful, was it?' Blue eyes taunted her, drawing a soft flush to her cheeks. His hold lessened and she was able to break free of his restraining arm. 'Though I was hoping for a little more enthusiasm from my fiancée. Guess we'll just have to work on it.'

She stared at him. Stark raving mad! And yet he looked so sane; there was no hint of weakness in the harsh planes of his tanned face, the square, stubborn chin. Nor could she ignore the unmistakable air of authority which this man exuded like his own personal musk, and which was wholly in contradiction to his wet, dishevelled appearance.

'What are you talking about?' Finally she managed to find her voice.

'You tell me, sweetheart,' he drawled. 'You're the one who just announced I was your fiancé.' The corners of the straight, firm mouth quirked upwards. 'Tell me, are we going to have a long engagement, or are you going to whisk me down the aisle any day now?'

The startling blue eyes gleamed with ill-surpressed mockery and Fern had the uncomfortable sensation of knowing that she was the butt of some joke which she didn't understand but which this stranger found immensely humorous. Why was she even standing here still, instead of making a hasty escape? A man who could so calmly go up to an unknown woman and kiss her might be capable of anything. But she seemed to be rooted to the spot, and in that moment came the instinctive certainty that this man would not harm her physically.

Then, to her intense irritation, he abruptly threw back his dark head and laughed, his teeth strong and white in the tanned, rugged face.

'OK, so what's the big joke?' Fern demanded icily.

'This is no joke, sweetheart, believe me.'

She ignored the irksome endearment once again, unable to place the slight, unfamiliar accent in the deep voice. He continued to study her and then he sighed and began to speak in a slow, deliberate voice as if addressing a child.

'You're engaged to the owner of this land?'

She nodded curtly, a bell clamouring in her head telling her that she ought to know the answer to this puzzle.

'That's me.' He extended a hand tauntingly. 'Piers Warrender.'

Fern absorbed the words in silence, ignoring the outstretched hand. Was this really David's half-brother, the product of their father's first marriage? The name was not new to her. David had mentioned him fleetingly once before, but his vivid description of the weak, ineffectual boy who had left Crofters over eighteen years ago at the age of seventeen, not even bothering to return for his father's funeral, did not match up with the broad-shouldered man with the strong, arresting face.

'This estate belongs to David Warrender,' Fern stated with a firmness she was far from feeling, but she was determined that he shouldn't even suspect at her hesitancy. Unconsciously her eyes searched the area around them. Surely he had a shirt somewhere, unless he made a habit of roaming around the countryside bare-chested as well as barefoot. The expanse of hard male skin troubled her, made her uneasy, although she refused to analyse why exactly.

'Is that what he told you?' He gave another of his irritating grins. He probably did toothpaste ads for a living, Fern thought with a viciousness that startled her, and she recognised that it was his aura of complete and utter self-assurance that she found so infuriating, contrasting as it did with her own thin veneer of confidence. 'He's jumping the gun a bit,' he continued in a lazy drawl. 'By one week, to be exact.'

'Can't you ever talk in anything but riddles?' Fern demanded in exasperation, her eyes finally coming to rest on a blue denim shirt, slung casually over a branch on the further bank. She could hardly insist that he swim over and retrieve the garment straight away, she supposed, envisaging his scornful amusement if she did so. She turned her attention back to him, fixing her eyes on a point somewhere above a gleaming, powerful shoulder.

He shrugged. 'Guess as you'll soon be part of the family, you might say you're an interested party. The estate was left to me by my father.' Fern was taken aback by the harshness that had crept into his voice. ' On condition that I returned within five years of his death to live here permanently. Deadline next Wednesday.'

She shook her head incredulously. It sounded too melodramatic to even contemplate . . . and yet she knew it was true, just as she had accepted that this man was who he claimed to be. Slowly, the implication of his words sunk in.

'You mean David has run the estate on his own for the past five years and you can just calmly waltz in like this and take it over?'

'Life's tough, isn't it?' he drawled, raking a lean hand through the unruly, dark hair.

'But it's so unfair!' Fern exploded. Whatever her personal

reservations about David, she respected his business acumen, knew of the long hours he put in to ensure that the estate ran smoothly and at a profit. She knew, too, of the deep love he had for his home and land.

'Your loyalty is touching.' The blue eyes suddenly and without warning narrowed into cold, hard blocks of ice. 'Bit of a shock to find you're no longer marrying a rich man, hm?'

To her dismay, Fern felt the colour surge into her face and knew that she must look the picture of guilt. And she deserved to, she admonished herself bitterly, for those traitorous moments when she had seriously contemplated marrying David, knowing that it would only be for the material advantages he could offer Carrie.

'I . . . ' she started defensively, and faltered at the look of contempt on his face.

'Don't worry,' he sneered, 'I shan't kick David out on to the streets straight away.' The callous indifference in his voice cut through Fern like a knife. 'Dare say I might even keep him on as manager. It'll be a bit of a come-down being the wife of a paid employee, won't it?'

Without her being fully conscious of her intended action, Fern's hand flew up, but he caught her wrist before she could deliver the stinging blow to the hard, cynical face.

'Guess I scored a bull's eye.' Disdainfully, he released her wrist from its searing grasp, turned abruptly away and moved with long, swift strides to the edge of the bank. He executed a perfect dive into the water and started swimming with crisp, powerful strokes towards the opposite bank.

Fern didn't wait to see him emerge but hastily began tracing her steps back towards the estate office. The meandering river tow-path had lost all its attractions; all she now longed to do was reach the sanctuary of Thyme Cottage as quickly as possible by the most direct route.

Breathlessly, she slowed down, realising that she had broken into a jog, and the knowledge that she was running away from Piers Warrender fuelled the smouldering anger that was directed not just at her antagonist but at herself. Why had she allowed herself to become so incensed by his insinuations when the dictates of common sense and dignity had demanded that she simply ignore him and walk away? That ineffectual attempt to slap his face had been totally out of character and had only served to increase his suspicions, suspicions, she realised wryly, that would doubtless be confirmed when she broke off her engagement to David. Oh, God, why had she been so witless as to have allowed him to kiss her? Jerkily, she rubbed the back of her hand across her lips as if by doing so she could eradicate the memory of that hard mouth on hers forever.

She pushed open the wooden gate and walked up the paved path to the solid two-bedroomed Victorian cottage that had been home for the past two years. She paused, gazed up at the small, sashed windows and frowned. If it was true that Piers had returned to claim his inheritance — and she knew that it would be deluding herself to hope otherwise — then strictly speaking he was now her employer—and, even more alarming, he owned the very roof over her head.

With growing unease, Fern contemplated the future. She knew she was highly competent at her job; Piers would have no grounds for dismissing her on that account. But she didn't doubt for a second but that a man who could appear out of the blue and, with no apparent remorse, cruelly disrupt the lives of his family would have no compunction about making life intolerable for a secretary he no longer wished to employ. Unwillingly, Fern started to grin. Wasn't she being somewhat over-pessimistic, letting her imagination run riot and creating problems before they even materialised?

It was unnaturally quiet inside the cottage, with no Carrie thundering around with her non-stop chatter, and Fern was surprised at how much she missed her after only a day's separation. A smile flickered over her face as she recalled the six-year old's excitement at the prospect of having tea and then spending the night with her current 'best friend'.

It was cool in the red-tiled hall after the oppressive heat outside and, beginning to shiver, Fern hurried up the narrow stairs to her bedroom, overlooking the large, rambling back garden. She stripped off her damp clothes and made her way along the landing to the small, old-fashioned bathroom, and sat on the edge of the enamel bath as it filled up with steaming water, contemplating the evening ahead without much enthusiasm. Had Piers been on his way up to Crofters when she'd encountered him, or had he already completed his mission? Her stomach muscles contracted. Would he be present at the dinner party tonight?

She felt too edgy to enjoy what had been intended as a long, leisurely soak, and after washing the river water from her hair and body she returned to her bedroom, wrapped in her towelling robe.

She opened her wardrobe and inspected the limited choice on offer, finally selecting a dark calf-length skirt and a demure silver-grey blouse. It was hardly summer wear, but her only summer dresses were hopelessly out of date. Her clothes, Fern mused, were undeniably dreary and unadventurous, but definitely practical and 'safe'. She brushed her damp hair vigorously so that it fell in a thick cascade of rich brown waves over her shoulder, and as she glimpsed her reflection in her dressing-table mirror her eyes darkened, memory stirring. Then her mouth tightened and deliberately she pulled her hair ruthlessly from her face and wound it into its neat coil.

Without Carrie to hinder her progress, she was ready

far too early, and so she elected to walk up to Crofters. David would doubtless escort her home in the dark later on.

There was only one car parked on the gravel crescent drive in front of the house. Either the dinner party was to be a small one or she was one of the first to arrive, Fern decided, and then frowned as she observed the name of a national hire-car firm imprinted on the solitary blue saloon. The car could only belong to Piers Warrender, she judged quickly, and was unprepared for the way her heartbeat quickened. Anyone would think she was afraid to meet him again, she thought, resenting her body's betrayal.

'Good evening, John,' she greeted the silver-headed man who opened the door to her, and was puzzled by the fleeting look of surprise in the pale grey eyes. He took the jacket she carried and led her across the wide marble floor.

'Mr Warrender is in his study,' he informed her, and Fern decided that she must have imagined the barely perceptible smirk that he bestowed upon her. John never smiled. She gave him a quick, searching glance but his face wore its habitual dour expression. Vaguely, she wondered why David should be in his study and not the lavishly furnished drawing-room where guests were normally entertained before dinner.

There were two men in the study standing by an open window, too intent with their harsh argument to notice her entrance immediately, and in that moment Fern willed herself to be anywhere else on earth but where she stood. She was utterly appalled to realise that she had been so preoccupied with the possible effects that Piers Warrender was going to have on her life that she hardly considered the far more devastating effect his homecoming would have on David and his mother. How could she have been so insensitive as to assume that the dinner party would go ahead tonight as if nothing untoward had happened? With uncomfortable insight, she was forced to recognise how insular she had become over the past years, determinedly cocooning herself in her small, safe world into which only Carrie was ever permitted.

Quietly, she turned round, intent on making her escape, but it was too late. The sudden silence in the room indicated that both men realised they now had an audience.

'Fern!' David strode to her side and for a second stared at her with blank eyes before comprehension dawned. 'The dinner party! Fern, I'm sorry, it's been cancelled.'

A wave of compassion flooded her as she witnessed the tension of his white, drawn face, and her eyes darkened as they flickered over to the tall figure, now leaning casually against the brick fireplace. He hadn't even changed, she noted, observing the dusty denim jeans and shirt disdainfully. Perhaps he didn't possess a change of clothing, she thought witheringly, and judging by the blue stubble on his square chin and the unruliness of his dark hair he didn't own a razor or comb either. She jolted as her eyes encountered the searing blue gaze, their cynical, cold glitter in total contradiction to the relaxed, indolent posture.

Quickly she turned her attention back to David.

'I should have telephoned you, Fern, but——'

'It's all right,' she cut in, not wanting him to make the humiliating admission that he had forgotten her entire existence in front of their observer. 'I'll go on home,' she added quietly and saw the look of unmistakable relief pass across his face. If she had been in love with David, how hurt she would have been to discover how little was his need of her in a time of crisis.

'Well, aren't you going to introduce me to your unlucky

dinner guest?' the familiar voice drawled. He had taken a silent step towards them, hand outstretched, and this time Fern had little option other than to take hold of it.

'Fern Maynard, Piers Warrender.' From a long way away, Fern heard David's stiff, unwilling voice make the formal introductions, only conscious of the disturbing sensation of those lean, hard fingers pressing against her soft palm.

'How do you do, Mr Warrender?' she murmured coolly, wondering why she was carrying on with this absurdity. Why hadn't she told David immediately that she'd already had the misfortune to meet his half-brother, that she knew the reason for the appalling tension in the room.

'Piers, please.' The deep voice mocked back at her. 'Haven't we met before?' he continued after a slight pause, assuming an expression of deep concentration, eyebrows knitted in a black line across his forehead. 'You seem so familiar. Now, where can it have been? Montreal? Oslo?'

'I have never been to either city,' she returned evenly. She was determined that he shouldn't ruffle her, but nor was she going to play this ridiculous game any longer. 'David, Mr Warrender and I——'

'No, I can see I was mistaken,' his voice cut through her attempted admission. 'You bear no resemblance at all to the girl I was thinking of.' His eyes swept over her slowly and deliberately, their expression insulting, and it took every ounce of control to fight the surge of colour to her face. It was easy to guess at the contrast he was making between the half-naked girl with the long, flowing hair, and the prim, upright figure with the set face before him now. 'But surely you'll stay for dinner now you're here?' he continued, and Fern frowned, utterly confused by the sudden polite concern in his voice, the light smile on his lips.

'Thank you, but—' Cautiously, she started to refuse the invitation, suspicious of the motive in extending it, but was once again interrupted. Was he incapable of allowing anyone else to finish their sentence? she wondered irritably.

'It'll be no trouble, will it, David? Perhaps you would ask John to lay an extra place?'

As Fern registered the open challenge in his voice, everything became clear. With revulsion, she realised that she was being used as a pawn in some egotistical power game in which Piers was indulging, confirming his position as master of Crofters.

'No, thank you.' Her words were adamant but quietly spoken, and her face remained an expressionless mask, but it was impossible to conceal the animosity from her eyes as they gazed squarely up at the dark man. Hadn't he inflicted enough on David already, stripping him of his home and land, without this added humiliation?

'Well, at least stay and have a drink before you go.' He smiled casually down at her, apparently immune to her hostility.

'Fern doesn't drink.'

With a jolt, Fern heard David's voice and realised that she had momentarily forgotten his presence completely; her whole attention had been concentrated on the one dominating figure to the exclusion of everything else.

'How very commendable.' Blue eyes rested tauntingly on the slim, brown-haired girl and then looked over her head as the door opened and John entered and approached David.

'Mrs Warrender wishes to see you in her living-room, sir.'

'Thank you, John.' David cast a swift, agitated look in Fern's direction. 'I'll see you tomorrow.'

She nodded, forcing a reassuring smile to her lips and

was immediately aware that with his departure she would be left alone with Piers, a state of affairs she had no wish to prolong.

'Not walking out on me, Miss Maynard?' He guessed her intention as she moved towards the door.

She flicked him a glance over her shoulder. 'Mrs Maynard,' she corrected shortly, and had the brief satisfaction of seeing the momentary disconcertment on his face. But her satisfaction was short-lived.

'Are you contemplating bigamy, by any chance, or has the unfortunate Mr Maynard already been disposed of?'

Was that supposed to be humorous? she thought distastefully.

'I'm a widow,' she explained curtly, and instinctively braced herself for the platitudes that always followed this admission. She reached out for the door-handle.

'How very convenient,' the voice drawled behind her.

It was impossible not to spin round and stare at him, impossible to believe that she had heard the callous words.

'Why the look of shock?' he enquired conversationally. 'If you're contemplating marrying my brother, you're hardly the grieving widow.' He paused and raised a dark eyebrow. 'Though, judging by the widow's weeds, I may have misjudged the situation.'

Fern didn't wait to hear any more. She opened the door and marched out into the hall, not bothering to wait for John to appear and retrieve her jacket, just desperate to get outside into the fresh air, to go anywhere as long as it was as far away from Piers Warrender as possible.

The huge wooden front door wouldn't budge. She tugged at it ferociously, to no avail.

'Allow me, Mrs Maynard.'

She had no option other than to stand aside and let him

pull it open. 'Always used to get stuck,' he commented.

She didn't bother to thank him. Why bother with the common courtesies? He didn't warrant them.

Swiftly, she moved through the front door and down the wide steps to the gravelled crescent drive.

'No car?' he murmured, following her outside. 'I'll give you a lift home.'

'I prefer to walk.'

'Sounds delightful,' he smiled amiably, matching his steps to hers, his intention obvious. Automatically Fern increased her pace, knowing as she did so how futile it was.

'Run marathons in your spare time?' he asked conversationally, and Fern ignored him.

Why was he deliberately trying to antagonise her like this? Their antipathy was mutual; she had no illusions that he desired her company any more than she did his. So why didn't he just leave her alone?

'Unusual for a man to forget that his fiancée is coming to dinner.' He broke the silence with a pretended thoughtfulness that in no way deceived Fern.

She kept her eyes firmly on the lane ahead. She might have guessed that sooner or later he was bound to bring this up, using it as further ammunition with which to taunt her. But she was determined that he wouldn't break her composure; she wouldn't give him the satisfaction of losing her temper, though why he was trying so hard to provoke it, she couldn't begin to comprehend. Perhaps he just enjoyed causing trouble, she thought scathingly.

'So when's the happy day?'

She had decided to ignore the question when an uncomfortable thought struck her. It would be typical of this man to make some caustic comment to Annette about the supposed wedding, making matters even more complicated than they were already.

'We haven't actually set a date yet,' she admitted curtly, and sighed inwardly. 'Actually, ' she tried to sound nonchalant, 'David and I haven't told anyone else yet.' That had been the one consolation. At least David would suffer no loss of face when she broke off the engagement, something she knew instinctively would be important to him.

'I'm touched to be your only confidant,' he commented sardonically. 'And how long have you known David?'

'Mind your own damn business!' The question had been innocuous enough, but something inside Fern just snapped without warning, all her good intentions evaporating. He wasn't interested in her or David; anything she said would simply be twisted and thrown back mockingly in her face. 'I've had enough of you for one day.' For a lifetime. She swung in front of him, eyes dark in her white, tense face. 'Go back to Crofters. Go to hell for all I care! Just leave me alone.' All the taunts she had endured raced through her mind. He was the most callous, cold-blooded bastard . . . Shaken, she realised that she had uttered those words aloud; she heard the rising shrillness in her voice and was appalled by the sensation of being so nearly out of control.

'Tsk, tsk, Mrs Maynard.' His eyes gleamed with brilliant blue flames, his amusement incensing her again. 'You'd better wash your mouth out with carbolic soap before you see David again.'

The colour inched into her face, burning her cheeks, and she bit her bottom lip. His comment was so apt. How on earth could he know David so well after all these years apart? Vividly, she recalled the day in the office when, having spilled the entire contents of the in-tray on to the floor, she had muttered a very mild oath under her breath. David's outrage would have done credit to the primmest of Victorian mamas. She felt as if she were going to choke . . . it was impossible, she couldn't stop it. Her eyes crinkled up and she started to laugh helplessly.

'Be quiet!'

She was stunned into silence, unable to believe that she had heard the sharp reproof. How could anyone be so impossibly ill-mannered? How dared he . . . ? She opened her mouth to protest, raised rebellious eyes to his face and stopped, confused. He wasn't even looking at her, but over her head to a point in the distance, the blue eyes intense and concerned. Instinctively, she turned round to see the object of his scrutiny and her stomach lurched.

'Oh, no,' she murmured quietly, her eyes wide with distress. And then she started to run.

CHAPTER TWO

A HAND gripped her shoulder, forcing her to a walk.

'Slowly,' the deep voice ordered her quietly.

Fern didn't protest, knew that Piers was right, her eyes never straying from the panic-stricken doe, who was trying vainly to free her nearside hind leg from the wire fencing that separated the lane from the arable land beyond.

Later, Fern couldn't remember why she had allowed Piers to take control, why she had trusted him so implicitly, obeying his command to soothe the terrified creature while he stooped down by its haunches.

It seemed an imposssible task at first. Despite Fern's desperate attempts to quieten and restrain her, the doe would not keep still, flailing her hind legs, driving the trapped one deeper and deeper into the ensnaring wire. Then, perhaps due to delayed shock, the doe lowered her head apathetically and offered no more resistance. Hardly daring to breathe in case she startled the doe again, Fern riveted her attention to Piers, watching the lean, strong hands as he deftly but gently began to ease the fragile leg back through the wire.

'Is it broken?' She forced the muffled whisper, dreading the reply, knowing the inevitable remedy should the answer be in the affirmative.

'She's lucky, just surface scratches.' He rose to his feet in a slow, controlled movement and took a careful step backwards. The doe remained motionless for a second, then raised her Y-shaped head, scented the air and bounded silently on down the lane towards the open forest.

Fern's mouth curved, her eyes glowing as she paid a silent

tribute to the animal's beauty. She knew that David, in common with most of the local farmers, regarded the roe deer as little more than a pest, but she never failed to fall under their spell, enchanted by their effortless grace.

'They can't resist the corn,' she murmured wistfully, and flicked a glance at the still figure by her side, exploring the harsh profile, suddenly curious to know what he was thinking. He must have sensed her scrutiny because, catching her off guard, he abruptly turned his head towards her. His smile was so unexpected that Fern's stomach muscles contracted involuntarily and she found herself grinning back. Her eyes met and locked into the blue ones, and in their dark depths she saw the echoes of her own delighted relief. He really cared about the doe, she thought, startled by the knowledge that he had shared her emotions.

'Ever tried venison sausages? There used to be a shop in Lyndhurst that . . . '

The smile was torn from her lips as she tried to block out his words, the cool indifference in his voice disillusioning her instantly. He was incapable of caring about anything, incapable of taking anything seriously, she recognised with disgust, admitting how mistaken she had been to think, even for a second, that this man had any redeeming qualities.

She appraised him disdainfully, unconsciously frowning as for the first time she noticed the crimson stain seeping through the sleeve of his denim shirt.

'You've cut your arm,' she said curtly. Probably not seriously, unfortunately. But the wire had been rusty, she reminded herself reluctantly. 'You'd better come back home and bathe it.'

He quirked a dark eyebrow. 'How can I possibly refuse such a gracious invitation,' he murmured drily.

Fern shrugged, and started walking homewards, not caring that he had guessed at her unwillingness to have him inside her home, not caring if he followed her or not.

'You live here?' he asked as she opened the gate of the cottage, the last few hundred yards having been traversed in a stony silence that he hadn't attempted to break.

There was a speculative gleam in his eye that she didn't trust. What was going through that warped mind? Did he think that David had set her up in some convenient love-nest?

'The cottage goes with the job,' she said swiftly. 'I'm David's secretary.' She turned towards him, blocking the path, and raised her eyes challengingly to his face. 'And I've heard the one about the secretary and her boss,' she said icily. If he dared make one crack, one snide insinuation, she'd run up to the front door and slam it shut in his face. Let him get blood poisoning, tetanus . . . It didn't help to know from the way the corners of the straight mouth quirked that he had once again guessed her thoughts correctly and was merely amused by her antipathy.

She opened the front door and walked briskly through the hall to the kitchen at the far end, acutely conscious of the masculine presence behind her. The sooner this was over, the better.

'Sit down,' she told him brusquely, indicating the wooden stool placed next to the round table, and moved across to the sink, running warm water into the red bowl. She retrieved a bottle of antiseptic and spilled some into the water. Cotton wool, she reminded herself, and rummaged around in the first-aid box attached to the cream wall.

She'd always supposed the kitchen to be of an average size—certainly it was large enough for herself and Carrie. But now it suddenly seemed claustrophobic, dominated by the male figure resting indolently on the stool, long legs stuck out in front of him.

Gritting her teeth, she carried the bowl over to the table.

'Do you want me to take off my shirt?' He raised a dark eyebrow at her. 'Or would it distract you from your tender ministration?

'Just roll up your sleeve,' she retorted with a briskness she was far from feeling. 'I'd hate you to catch pneumonia as well as lockjaw,' she added with saccharine sweetness. Arrogant was an understatement, she thought witheringly. Did he think she was going to fall into a swoon at the sight of an exposed male chest? She felt her cheeks heat, traitorously remembering her earlier agitation by the river, the disturbing effect of that lean male body. Bending her head quickly to avoid the all too discerning gaze, she soaked a wad of cotton wool in the bowl, and then hesitated, her eyes concentrated on the golden arm lain on the table, the blood beginning to congeal around the jagged weal. Come on, she admonished herself, think of the countless times you've patched up Carrie's cut knees.

But this was different, she thought uneasily as her fingers touched the warm male skin. It was impossible not to be aware of the hard band of muscle beneath her touch, impossible not to notice the sheen of dark hairs, the same colour as those which ran the length of his chest . . .

'Ouch,' he grimaced. 'For God's sake, woman, I've only got one right arm, and I was planning to keep it for a while longer!'

'Don't call me woman!' Fern snapped, almost grateful for the flare of anger, an antidote to the nervousness that had caused her to be so clumsy. She tossed the cotton wool in the bowl, deliberately spraying him with water. 'You can damn well do it yourself.'

That had been childish, she rebuked herself instantly, irritated that she had allowed him to needle her so successfully. She leant against the sink and watched with narrowed grey eyes as, whistling under his breath, he continued bathing the wound himself.

He rolled down the shirt-sleeve and raised his head.

'Thank you,' he murmured with an exaggerated politeness that set Fern's teeth on edge, indicating that he had finished with the bowl.

Was that smile supposed to disarm her? she wondered scornfully, meeting the dazzling blue eyes equably. She picked up the bowl and emptied the contents down the sink. 'Wouldn't be a bad idea to have a tetanus jab,' she said briskly. With any luck he'd make a rapid departure and hurry down to the local surgery.

'Had a shot before I left New Zealand,' he returned laconically.

She absorbed the words in silence, drying her hands on a towel, keeping her back towards him. New Zealand. Perhaps that would explain the barely perceptible accent. Was that where he'd spent the last eighteen years? Doing what exactly? She frowned, staring out of the kitchen window without consciously registering the garden beyond. She couldn't imagine him sitting behind a desk all day, confined to an office, having already gauged just how deceptive was that air of casual inertia. There wasn't an ounce of fat on his body, no suggestion of too many over-long business lunches. It was impossible anyway to visualise him dressed formally in a suit. His every movement, the lithe, loping walk, the deeply tanned skin—all were indicative of a man accustomed to physical exertion and an outdoor life. Yet his hands, Fern recalled, although strong and lean, had been free of the hard calluses normally associated with manual labour. For heaven's sake! She brought herself up sharply. Why was she indulging in this pointless speculation? She wasn't interested in Piers Warrender's past or his future!

She shot a glance over her shoulder and her mouth tightened. Do make yourself at home, she thought acidly. He had exchanged the stool for a chair, leaning back into it, hands folded idly behind his dark head, the buttons of the denim shirt stretched almost to breaking-point across the powerful chest. One leg was crossed casually over a knee, the jeans taut along the line of the muscular thigh. Fern's mouth curled derisively. Macho man himself —even down to the designer stubble on the tenacious jaw. Some women, she admitted reluctantly, might find his blatant, overt masculinity attractive, might even regard it as a challenge, but it left her cold. That knotted sensation in the pit of her stomach was due to hunger, she assured herself confidently.

He was surveying the kitchen with an almost proprietorial air. Anyone would think he owned the damn place, she thought irritably, and jolted. He did, she reminded herself uneasily. She followed his gaze as his eyes rested on the bright crayon drawings stuck to the cupboard, moved to the small blue wellington boots by the back door, and then flickered over to the dresser where she had placed the most recent of Carrie's school photographs. He studied the image of the small brown-haired girl with wide grey eyes and an engaging grin and lifted a quizzical dark eyebrow at Fern.

She could ignore the unspoken question, she supposed, but it seemed simpler to volunteer the information now rather than have to correct his mistaken assumption later on.

'My niece,' she said quietly and was confused by the sudden unguarded expression in his eyes. Not a reflection of his surprise that he had doubtlessly drawn the wrong conclusion about her relationship to Carrie, but something else . . . no . . . the expression was gone, had been too fleeting for her to analyse properly.

'She lives with you?'

Fern turned to face him squarely, unconscious of her defensive stance, an instinctive reaction to the suspicious gentleness in his voice. 'My sister died when Carrie was a baby. I've looked after her ever since.'

'And how does Carrie's father fit into all this?'

'Katherine wasn't married,' she answered shortly. This was the moment she most hated, the explanations that never failed to revive memories that were not truly dormant. 'Won't you be late for dinner?' Hardly a subtle hint, but who cared? She wasn't going to pursue this conversation any longer.

He gave her the by now familiar mocking grin, but to her relief rose to his feet with catlike agility. 'Think I'll be missed?'

'I doubt it,' she returned tartly, and for the first time found herself wondering what it must feel like to come home after eighteen years and discover how unwelcome was your return. But then what did he expect under the circumstances, she concluded scathingly—the fatted calf? She certainly wasn't going to waste any sympathy on Piers Warrender.

Deliberately she moved across to the back door and held it wide open.

'Goodnight, Mrs Maynard.' Blue eyes raked her face as he passed by. 'Thank you for your hospitality.'

She scowled up at him. If that remark was supposed to make her feel awkward because she had not even bothered to offer him a cup of coffee, he was out of luck.

'See you in the office tomorrow.' His voice was no longer lazy but crisp and authoritative. 'Nine o'clock sharp.'

Fern's scowl deepened, her whole being bristling with resentment and intense irritation at the implication in the dictatorial voice that she was prone to tardiness. If he was seriously intending to take over the running of the estate— and her heart dropped at the prospect—someone should advise him to attend a course on managerial skills—with particular emphasis on staff relations.

'And for God's sake try and smile in the morning. Unfortunately I don't share David's penchant for sour-faced females.'

It took a second for the words to sink in, and a moment longer for the retaliatory words to form in her head, by which time it was too late. He had disappeared around the side of the cottage and she heard the click of the wooden gate closing behind him.

Unconsciously, Fern had taken a step into the back garden, the evening air cool against her flushed, furious face. Her hands were clenched into fists by her side, her teeth gritted together in an effort to swallow the epithets she longed to shout out after him. Why did he make her so angry? She couldn't remember when she'd last lost her temper, and yet ever since she'd encountered Piers Warrender she'd had to fight every inch of the way to keep it in check. Was he so damned offensive to everyone, or had she been singled out for the honour?

She took a deep, controlling breath and turned back into the cottage. She wasn't going to waste her time trying to psychoanalyse a man like him. She wasn't even going to think about him. Determinedly she marched into the living-room, switched on the light, drew the dark green curtains and walked across the shabby, worn carpet to the ancient sofa, surprisingly comfortable despite its dilapidated appearance. She curled up her legs under her and picked up the half-finished novel lying on the coffee-table beside her. After a few moments she put the book down with a heavy sigh. It was hopeless; she couldn't relax, couldn't concentrate. Her mind was a confused whirlpool of fragmented half-sentences, broken up by the image of a dark, mocking face.

Restlessly, she sprang to her feet, glancing ruefully at the clock on the mantelpiece. It was too early to go to bed; she'd never sleep. The only antidote to her present mood was activity, she decided resolutely. She might just as well make the most of Carrie's absence and tidy up her room, a chore long overdue. She dashed upstairs, changed swiftly into a pair of jeans and a sweatshirt, and, armed with a duster and vacuum cleaner, entered the smaller of the two bedrooms, eyeing the disorder without much enthusiasm.

Oh, God, she didn't want to work for Piers Warrender! She sat down on the edge of the single bed, eyes dark with despondency. It would be intolerable having to spend eight hours a day in his company. How uncomplicated life had seemed in comparison that morning, with just David to worry about. Sighing, she slid from the bed and dropped to her knees, picking up the miniature farm animals strewn across the carpet and depositing them in the wooden farmyard. Carrie was settled at the school in the village, had made friends . . . she couldn't uproot her yet again. Fern rose to her feet, her face set. She must try and stick out her job, at least give it a chance. Perhaps Piers would be different in a working environment. Surely, anyway, he'd soon become bored with baiting her if she failed to respond to his gibes and simply ignored his insulting remarks?

After all, nothing he said could possibly wound her, could it? And he would have to acknowledge that she was more than capable of carrying out her duties ... even if they didn't include grinning inanely at him all day!

She moved over to the white dressing-table by the window and started to dust the top absently, and then paused. Slowly she picked up the framed photograph and stared down at it with shadowed eyes. Katherine, two years her senior, grave-faced with only the faintest glimmer of a smile at the corners of her mouth. It was the only one of her sister that Fern had had in her possession to give to Carrie. Her eyes moved across the photograph to the second girl portrayed, a girl in a scarlet sun-dress, with an animated face, laughing up at the photographer. Herself at nineteen, shortly before her marriage, two terms at university successfully completed. A year later and her whole world had collapsed; she'd been widowed, Kathy was dead and she'd had no option other than to drop out of university to take care of Carrie.

Fern shook her head. Impossible to believe now that the girl with sparkling, challenging eyes had ever existed ... had been transformed seven years later into a sour-faced female clad in widow's weeds. She tried to laugh, but the sound came out as a strangled choke, her throat constricting painfully. Piers' words had shaken her, she admitted for the first time. Her anger had been a camouflage for the raw flick of hurt.

Eyebrows drawn together, Fern placed the photograph back in position and turned towards the window, gazing out into the twilight, the last rays of sun slipping behind the huge coniferous trees at the end of the garden. Of course she'd changed over the years! Who hadn't? But in her case, she reminded herself uneasily, the change had been deliberate. She'd consciously chosen to dress and act in a manner guaranteed not to draw attention to herself. She'd avoided any situation which might make emotional demands upon her, avoided any confrontations in which she might have to assert herself, always opting for the easier, more passive course. Hence her present predicament with David, she thought with self-disgust. Hadn't she only agreed to go out with him in the first place because she'd known she was in no danger of falling in love with him? She'd deliberately chosen to live her life in a vacuum, insulated in her own private world, determined never to trust or become dependent on anyone ever again.

'Damn you, Piers Warrender,' she suddenly muttered vehemently under her breath. It was he who had prompted this tortuous self-analysis. Involuntarily, she shuddered, an irrational pinprick of fear crawling up her spine. Her eyes widened, aghast with shocked revelation. She was frightened of Piers, felt threatened by something she didn't understand. Grimly, she dismissed the notion as absurd, and determinedly marched over to the vacuum cleaner and switched it on, the noise deterring any more soul searching.

'Well, Mrs Maynard, you look almost human!'

Fern ignored the caustic remark, pretending that she hadn't heard the deep, mocking voice. Her eyes remained fixed steadily ahead, her hands gripped over the edge of the seat as the Land Rover bumped erratically down the gravelled track.

Piers had insisted on folding back the canvas roof of the Land Rover, and the wind had tugged some of the silky brown hair from its neat pleat, and whipped at her cheeks, flaming her clear skin with colour. Irritably, Fern pushed back the soft tendrils of hair that framed her face, disliking the feel of the stray wisps hanging down her neck. Human! It was hardly the adjective she would have chosen. She felt hot, dishevelled, and—her eyes rested briefly on the huge wellingtons on her feet—utterly ridiculous.

It had never occurred to her that Piers would want a tour of the estate that morning, or insist that she accompany him, otherwise she would have come dressed in her jeans and her own wellingtons, instead of having to borrow the large pair always present in the back of the Land Rover. She knew from past experience that her open-toed flat sandals would be totally impractical for trudging through a muddy farmyard.

She had arrived to work promptly at nine o'clock and discovered Piers sprawled in the outer office, leaning back in the chair she considered to be her own, feet up on the desk.

'Where's David?' she had demanded curtly, not bothering with even the most cursory of greetings. Her eyes rested on the lean length disdainfully. Ye gods, this man was supposed to be her employer; someone she at least ought to respect if not necessarily like!

'Solicitor,' he answered laconically, not glancing up from the paper in which he was apparently engrossed, and a burst of elation swept over Fern. Perhaps David's lawyer had discovered a loophole in the will.

'Right, let's get going.' He had tossed the newspaper aside, interrupting her pleasant daydream in which David returned, victorious, and ordered his insufferable half-brother out of the office.

'Going where?' she enquired icily, resenting his high-handedness. He sounded like a marshal in an old-fashioned western, ordering his posse to get mounted. 'Do I get a deputy's badge?' she added sarcastically, and was taken aback by the flash of strong white teeth, disconcerted to realise that he was on the same wavelength as herself. She didn't smile back. She didn't want to share anything with this man, certainly not humour.

'I'd like to meet all the tenant farmers,' he explained, and Fern's mouth curved scornfully. She might have guessed that he would prefer going gallivanting around the countryside, playing lord of the manor, master of all he surveyed, to the more mundane chore of going through the accounts and paperwork, which she had assumed would be his first priority.

'They don't touch their fetlocks any more,' she murmured sweetly.

'How disappointing,' he returned drily, unfolding his long body from the chair.

The Land Rover jolted over a rut and Fern clung to the strap on the door, determined to keep a safe distance between herself and the man beside her. She'd already been thrown against the hard male form once, and she had no wish to repeat the disquieting experience. She had deliberately avoided looking directly up at him, but somehow she could see him anyway, the image of his face imprinted strongly in her mind, the blue eyes narrowed against the glare of the sun, the chiselled features, the straight, firm mouth, the cynicism only relieved when he smiled, the square, uncompromising jaw, clean-shaven today. The tang of male after-shave assailed her nostrils, mingled with the soapy scent of clean skin. He was wearing jeans again, but the denim shirt had been replaced by a black one that perversely made his hair look even darker, glinting with blue-black lights in the sunlight. Not a marshal, Fern dismissed her earlier analogy —they always wore white shirts. No, he would have been an outlaw in those bygone days, a man governed by his own rules and mores, dismissive of society's conventions. Probably a rustler, she concluded caustically, taking that which did not rightfully belong to him.

Fern tried to relax, to enjoy the sensation of the sun warm

on her skin, but she couldn't, her whole body remaining tense, alert to the slightest movement beside her. This man might be the epitome of everything she most abhorred in the male species but, she admitted reluctantly, it was impossible to ignore him. Her senses were tuned to a pitch she'd never experienced before, every inch of her acutely conscious of the dominant, masculine presence. A fierce wave of resentment exploded inside her; she didn't want to be so physically aware of this or any other man ever again.

Piers ground the Land Rover to a halt in front of a five-barred gate and turned his head, a dark eyebrow raised towards her. She might have guessed that there would be an ulterior motive for her presence, Fern thought grimly, strongly tempted to ignore the unspoken but ill-disguised order.

Clambering down from the Land Rover didn't pose too much of a problem, but returning to her seat after opening and closing the gate was a different matter. Her straight blue skirt hadn't been designed for such an activity, and it restricted her movement. The cumbersome boots weren't much assistance either. There was no alternative—unless she wanted to fall flat on her face—other than to hitch her skirt well up above her knees. Normally, she wouldn't have thought twice about it, but then normally the exposed length of her tanned legs weren't subject to quite such scrutiny. Hadn't he ever seen a pair of female legs before? she wondered acidly. He had certainly seen hers before, she reminded herself uneasily, remembering their first encounter by the river. That expression of undisguised interest in his eyes had been the same then.

'Voyeur!' she muttered under her breath, thankfully regaining her seat and pulling the skirt back down over her knees, not caring that, judging by the small, mocking smile tugging at the corners of his mouth, he judged the action old-maidish. She wasn't here to entertain him!

Fern stared straight ahead as the Land Rover roared back into life. Piers' insults might rankle, might conceivably wound her hitherto dormant feminine pride, but they were infinitely preferable to his admiration. The fact that he might find her attractive in any way, albeit it just her legs, didn't bear contemplation.

'How long have the Andersons been at Highwood Farm?' The idle drawl broke through her brooding silence as the Land Rover bumped over a cattle-grid.

'Five years.' The question restored her composure; this was something she could deal with. 'They're concentrating on building up a herd of pedigree Guernseys.' She began to elucidate, giving him detailed information about the working of the farm, all the facts and figures having been committed to memory, and then paused in disbelief. He was whistling, not paying her the courtesy of even pretending to listen. 'Am I boring you?' she asked stiffly, flicking him a baleful sideways glance.

'Yes,' he agreed, the blue eyes never straying from the farm track. 'Personally I've never found milk yields and fertilisers to be the most stimulating topics of conversation.'

'Then why bother to visit the farms?' she flared. 'Why bother to come back to England at all?' It was evident that he wasn't in the least interested in the estate, had no comprehension of the work involved in running it. And she hadn't once mentioned fertilisers.

He didn't reply, swung the Land Rover into the farmyard, jumped down agilely and strode towards the house. Fern stared after the tall, retreating figure. It was like water off a duck's back. Nothing she could ever say would penetrate that thick, insensitive skin. And he could have waited for her instead of charging ahead like that.

Some ten minutes later, Fern was in the large

farmhouse kitchen being plied with mugs of tea and huge wedges of home-made fruit cake, watching the female members of Tom Anderson's family, his wife and two daughters, being totally captivated by Piers. It was utterly nauseating, she decided, glaring down at the cake she had unconsciously crumbled up on her plate. She felt the farmer's eyes on her, flushed and hastily committed the small particles of cake to her mouth, where she had difficulty in swallowing them. Even the black and white collie, who normally gave her a wide berth, sat by Piers with its head on his knee, proving just how wrong was the old adage about animals and children. Tom, renowned for his dourness, was actually laughing at one of Piers' banal jokes. What on earth was the matter with everyone? Fern thought despairingly. Was she the only sane person in the room? The two girls were eyeing Piers as if they'd never seen a man before in their lives and Mrs Anderson was practically sidling up towards him? Couldn't they see through Piers, see beyond that insincere charm to the ruthless egotist beneath?

'How long will you be staying in England?' the farmer's wife asked. Her eyes had been avid with curiosity ever since Fern had made the brief introductions.

Fern leant back in her chair, waiting for the family's reaction to the news that Piers, a man who had no interest in farming, was their new landlord.

'I'm thinking of returning to live in England permanently,' he answered easily.

Fern choked into her mug of tea. Only thinking about it?

'All right, love?' Tom Anderson patted her vigorously on the back and she nodded, her eyes flying accusingly to Piers' face. What was he playing at now? Why hadn't he told them the truth instead of being so evasive?

Then she nearly choked again as the farmer and Piers launched into a highly technical discussion about modern farming methods which was way over her head. It was apparent from the look of growing respect in Tom Anderson's eyes that Piers knew exactly what he was talking about. The familiar spark of resentment surged over her. Once again she had been hoodwinked by his casual air . . . and she felt a fool. She flicked him a glance from under her dark lashes and saw that he was smiling at the elder of the two girls, a vivacious eighteen-year-old whose fresh-faced blonde looks evidently appealed to him.

'Have you brought your wife and family with you?' The girl's eyes were deliberately innocent, but her mouth curved provocatively.

Fern's head jerked upwards, unconsciously holding her breath. It had never ocurred to her that Piers might be married.

'I'm not married,' he murmured, meeting the girl's eyes, and Fern lowered her head quickly, frowning into her mug of tea. He was perfectly aware of the devastating effect he was having on the gullible girl, and loving every minute of it, she thought with disgust. She heard the teasing drawl and stiffened. He was quite openly flirting with the blonde now and, quite unexpectedly, Fern felt a twinge of envy at the assured ease with which the eighteen-year-old responded to his bantering remarks, confident in her ability to attract and hold male attention. Once, Fern realised with a sharp pang, she too had possessed that naïve confidence.

'Cradle-snatching one of your pastimes?' she found herself growling as they made their departure from the house, shuffling along in her wellingtons in an effort to keep up with Piers as they crossed the yard.

'Don't knock it,' he drawled and, catching Fern off guard,

reached out a hand and swung her round in front of him. He surveyed her indignant, flushed face with blue, insolent eyes. 'You know, a toy boy could be just what you need to get rid of some of those hang-ups.'

'You're disgusting,' she retorted icily, shrugging off the restraining hand contemptuously and climbing inelegantly up into the Land Rover. What hang-ups? No, she wasn't even going to think about the possible implications. It had been a shot in the dark by Piers, that was all, another example of his puerile attempts to shock her.

The midday sun beat down on Fern's head as the Land Rover bumped down the track away from Home Farm, their third and final port of call.

'Successful morning,' Piers murmured, glancing right as he pulled out into the main road that led back towards Crofters.

Fern didn't answer, gazing stonily ahead through the windscreen. As far as she was concerned the morning had been a complete waste of time, and she would have been far more profitably employed at the estate office. Vividly she recalled previous visits she had made to the farm with David. They had been business—not social—events, conducted formally, problems relating to the farms analysed and discussed. She smiled approvingly at the memory and then frowned uneasily. But never in the past, she was forced to admit, had she encountered such warm hospitality as she had met with today in Piers' company.

'Fancy having lunch in the pub over there?' The deep voice cut through her muddled thoughts.

'No, thanks,' she returned coolly, dismissing the invitation instantly, thinking longingly of the invigorating shower she intended to take back at the cottage during her lunch-hour.

'As you wish.' Almost before she had time to register what was happening, he had swung the Land Rover into the car park of the half-timbered public house, a popular haunt of local farmers on market day in the nearby town. 'Shan't be long,' he murmured, then sprang down from his seat and strode towards the beckoning doors of the inn, leaving Fern staring after him with wide, incredulous eyes.

Incredulity swiftly changed to slow, curdling anger. Never in her life had she been subjected to such appalling manners. He was . . . adjectives failed her. He hands clenched and unclenched by her side. What was she supposed to do for the next half-hour, possibly even an hour? Sit here like an idiot, baking in the sun? She grimaced. It was at least eight miles back to Crofters. It would take her hours to cover that distance on foot, encumbered by the huge wellingtons, and Piers would doubtless pass her on the road long before she had reached her goal, placing her in an even more humiliating position than she was already. If only he had left the keys in the ignition . . . if only it weren't so hot! She sighed ruefully accepting the inevitable and slid down from the Land Rover.

She spotted Piers immediately she entered the crowded lounge bar, the dark head and broad shoulders easily discernible above the throng.

'I've ordered two home-made steak and kidney puddings,' he greeted her with aggravating casualness as she reached his side, evincing no surprise at her appearance. He had been so sure of getting his own way, Fern realised with smouldering irritation, so certain that she would eventually follow meekly after him. Automatically she started to thank him, albeit ungraciously, and then compressed her lips firmly together, choking back the words. Had she become so feeble-minded that she was going to thank this man for ordering a lunch not of her choosing, over which she had not even been consulted? She gazed up at him.

'The fresh air must have given you quite an appetite,' she murmured sweetly. 'Personally, I've always found one portion perfectly sufficient.'

He quirked an eyebrow at her, but his eyes were shadowed, unreadable. It was impossible to gauge his thoughts, impossible to tell whether her minor rebellion had irked, or merely amused him.

'That'll be just one steak and kidney then, please,' he amended the order easily, smiling at the attentive barmaid. 'What would you like to drink, Fern?'

'I have a choice?' she muttered tartly, registering that it was the first time he had used her first name. 'Orange juice, please.' Deliberately she addressed the barmaid directly. 'And a salad sandwich,' she added decisively for good measure, and began to delve into her leather handbag.

'Lunch is on me,' Piers intervened, evidently guessing her intention. Fern ignored him and placed a handful of silver coins into the startled barmaid's hand. She turned to the dark-haired man. 'As I have no intention of ever reciprocating lunch, I should prefer to go Dutch,' she informed him briskly. She picked up her orange juice, wondering if it would have appeared quite so rapidly had she been alone. No, that was negative thinking, and she had been negative for far too long. 'I'll go and find a table,' she announced, moving away from the bar.

She slipped into a vacant seat near the door, conscious that she was trembling but even more aware of the swell of elation coursing through her. She couldn't remember when she had last asserted herself—and it had been a surprisingly satisfying experience. Her fingers curled around the stem of her glass. She felt more confident, more relaxed than she had all morning.

She glanced up as Piers joined her, amused to see how uncomfortable he looked as he curled his long frame into the restricted space opposite her.

'Why didn't you tell any of the tenants that you were their new landlord?' she demanded bluntly, voicing the question that had been nagging at her ever since they left the Andersons'. She would have expected him to relish dropping his bombshell on the unsuspecting farmers, and yet he had avoided the issue completely, responding evasively to any direct questions about his unexpected appearance at Crofters.

'Perhaps I haven't made up my mind yet.' He shrugged infuriatingly and took a long draught of beer.

'After only five years to consider it?' Fern scoffed. She didn't believe him for a second, unconvinced that a man as decisive as Piers would be prone to vacillation. No, he knew exactly what his plans were. This apparent hesitation was merely a new ploy with which to taunt David, to keep him on tenterhooks, build up his hopes only to dash them viciously at the last minute. The cruelty of the cat-and-mouse game appalled her—and seemed incomprehensible. If anyone should be feeling vindictive, surely it should be David under the circumstances, certainly not Piers, who was the victor. She took a sip of orange. How ironic it was that David had managed the estate quite so successfully. Had it been running at a loss, encumbered by heavy debts, she was sure Piers would not have even contemplated taking the estate over. His length of absence hardly suggested that he had formed any sentimental attachment to Crofters. No, the attraction for him was purely mercenary. She frowned reflectively. But how long would the estate continue to run at a profit with Piers at the helm? she wondered acidly. A new thought struck her.

'So while you're weighing up the pros and cons,' she murmured caustically, 'who in effect is in charge of the estate?' Or did he think it ran itself?

He smiled as the waitress appeared with their respective lunches and then turned his attention back to Fern. 'Until the legalities are completed next Wednesday, David.'

Fern's eyes narrowed. 'Does he know where I am this morning?' Had Piers informed him of his intention of visiting the farms with her?

'Not unless he's telepathic,' he returned easily. He looked down at his laden plate appreciatively. 'This looks good.'

Wonderful! Fern eyed her sandwich with less enthusiasm. So David would have expected to find her working diligently in the office on his return, and instead she was stuck here with his half-brother. She sighed, taking a bite of the sandwich. The whole situation was fast bordering on the farcical. Who, right now, was strictly her employer anyway? David or Piers? She flicked a glance at the latter from under her lashes and regretfully decided that the steak and kidney pudding did look far more appetising than her own more meagre choice.

They drew up in front of the estate office, the journey back having been conducted in silence, and Piers leapt out, disconcerting Fern by striding round to her side and offering up a mocking hand. She threw him a withering glance. It was a little late for such displays of gallantry, seeing that she had struggled unaided all morning.

Concentrating on avoiding his helping hand, she lost her footing and landed in an ungainly sprawl on the dusty ground. Immediately two strong arms lifted her to her feet.

'Thanks,' she muttered, acutely aware of his hands resting lightly either side of her waist. That new burst of confidence had been transitory, she realised uneasily. At this precise moment she felt as awkward and self-conscious as a teenager, and, worst of all, she felt inexplicably vulnerable. Quickly she started to turn away, but was immobilised as he moved his hands upwards and grasped her shoulders firmly. She started to protest, but her words were muffled by the hard, bruising mouth. Her hands pushed ineffectually against the solid wall of his chest and fell helplessly to her sides. She felt totally disorientated, oblivious to everything but the fierce scalding sensation teasing through her veins that drained all resistance from her.

The release was as abrupt as had been the onslaught, leaving Fern shaky, drawing erratic gulps of air into her lungs. Instinctively her eyes searched the craggy face . . . and she froze. His eyes were hard, disdainful as they scoured her flushed face. Then they lifted, looked over her head and a derisory smile tugged at the corners of the harsh, straight mouth.

Automatically Fern turned her head to follow his gaze and saw the angry, tense face staring at them out through the office window.

CHAPTER THREE

'HOW very subtle!' Fern muttered caustically as comprehension dawned. Piers had known that David was watching them from the office. His action hadn't been spontaneous, but contrived deliberatively to antagonise their observer. His kiss had been executed coldly, mechanically, and with as much feeling as if she'd been a lump of wood—and for one traitorous moment she had almost responded to that hard, warm, deceiving mouth. She felt sick at the thought, and equally determined that Piers should never suspect how close she had come to that final humiliation.

Her stomach muscles were cramped in a fierce knot. She wanted to lash out, protest at the way in which she had been used, but that would be playing straight into Piers' hands. She forced her stiff facial muscles into an expression of acute boredom. 'Next time you feel compelled to indulge in infantile games,' she murmured, her voice heavy with ennui, 'count me out.' Slowly and nonchalantly she turned away and began sauntering leisurely towards the estate office. This time she thought triumphantly, she'd had the last word, and then she faltered as she heard the low, mocking laugh echo behind her.

'How could you, Fern? Allow that man to touch you?' The fair-headed man paced furiously up and down the length of the office.

Fern sighed wearily, leaning back in her chair. If only they could have got this all over and done with the other day, had a blazing row and cleared the air. But David had preferred to

51

sulk for the last two days, not even speaking to her unless absolutely necessary. It wasn't until late this afternoon that he had finally exploded.

'Can't we just drop it now?' Fern asked quietly, patience ebbing fast. She wanted to put the whole incident out of her mind; this belated inquest would serve no purpose at all. She glanced at her watch and grimaced. 'I should have collected Carrie ten minutes ago.'

'You think I can just drop it?' David exclaimed, pausing in front of the desk to glare at Fern. 'Forget that I ever saw my fiancée being mauled about by another man?'

'He only kissed me, for heaven's sake,' Fern muttered, exasperated, and then frowned. Surely she wasn't defending Piers now, was she? But David's furious betrayed-husband routine was beginning to irritate her intensely. Right now there seemed little to choose between either of the Warrender men. And why should she be bearing the brunt of David's ill temper anyway, when logically his anger should have been directed at Piers? Except that the latter seemed to have conveniently disappeared from the face of the earth.

She hadn't seen him since parting from him in the courtyard two days ago, and judging from some of David's muttered comments it would appear that he had no idea of his half-brother's whereabouts either.

Fern raised her head, forcing her attention back to David and stiffened as she registered his words.

'After all, a man doesn't simply kiss a girl for no reason at all.'

'Are you implying that I encouraged him?' Fern enquired frostily. This really was the last straw! Why couldn't David see that the whole episode had been engineered by Piers to evoke exactly this reaction?

'Well you did spend all morning with him, tearing

around the countryside, alone together. What am I supposed to think?'

'Frankly, I don't care what you damn well think!' Fern flared and nearly laughed out loud at the expression of outrage and shock on the fair man's face.

'I don't know what's happened to you over the last few days,' he muttered petulantly. 'You've changed so much. You're not the girl I thought I knew at all.'

It had long baffled Fern why David should have ever wanted to marry her in the first place—certainly it wasn't because of some grand passion—but now she wondered why she hadn't understood his motives much sooner. They were so obvious. David wanted a wife who would be submissive, self-effacing, compliant, someone whom he could manipulate, who would never argue with him . . . and she had appeared to fit the bill. It was her own fault, Fern recognised guiltily. She had given him every reason to believe that his character analysis of her was correct. How disillusioned he must be feeling now to discover that she had feet of clay.

Fern swallowed, lifting her eyes to his. 'I think it would be best all round if we broke off the engagement,' she said quietly, bracing herself for his reaction.

He nodded. 'Under the circumstances, I am bound to agree.'

She blinked. It had all been so easy . . . she'd been steeling herself for weeks to say those words . . . and it had all been so unbelievably simple. She'd been convinced that there would be some repercussions, if only because she had taken the initiative and made the final decision. Yet David's voice had been calm and restrained.

'I'll see you at the Show tomorrow,' she murmured awkwardly, picking up her handbag as she rose to her feet. There seemed little point in prolonging this moment. 'I'll be down at the ground as soon as I've dropped Carrie off at the

Joneses'. She paused in the doorway. 'I'm sorry, David.' Sorry for not having been stronger right from the start.

He inclined his head slightly, acknowledging her remark, but didn't answer.

She felt an overwhelming sense of release as she stepped out into the fresh air, as if she were free at last from some huge burden. One problem resolved . . . now, if only Piers had vanished for good, life could return to normal. Peaceful, uneventful—and boring.

Mechanically, Fern opened the door of her ancient Mini and slipped into the driver's seat, her eyes dark and reflective. She might dislike Piers intensely but, she admitted uneasily, somehow he had managed to rouse her from the stupefying lethargy in which she had become immersed. He'd made her feel alive again. Her face troubled, Fern turned on the ignition and drove away from the estate.

'Why are you putting the plates in the fridge?' Carrie watched her aunt with interested eyes.

'What?' Fern stared down at the dinner plates in her hand and the half-opened fridge door. 'Silly me,' she murmured lightly, setting the plates down in their intended position on the kitchen table. She smiled into the small freckled face. 'Go and change out of your school clothes, darling. Supper won't be long.'

Carrie nodded and galloped from the room. It might not be a bad idea to hurry back and keep a vigilant eye on the supper preparations, she decided, thinking back to the cheese and strawberry jam sandwiches she'd discovered in her lunch box at dinnertime. And Aunt Fern had forgotten she needed her plimsolls for PE today. She chuckled. Perhaps her aunt might even forget to send her to bed tonight.

'Is there something wrong?' Fern asked gently, puzzled by the woebegone expression on her niece's face as she inspected the salad on her plate.

'No,' Carrie muttered, swallowed a piece of tomato and sighed mournfully. 'It's just salad, isn't it?' She took a mouthful of mashed potato and brightened, her eyes resting on Fern's face with delighted anticipation.

'I've put sugar in the potatoes, haven't I?' Fern swallowed her own mouthful and grinned, finding it impossible to ignore Carrie's infectious giggles. 'Let's just hope your dotty aunt hasn't put salt in the pudding,' she added drily. 'It's your favourite. Apple sponge.' What on earth was the matter with her tonight? No, not just tonight. She'd been like this for the past few days, as if she were in a trance, unable to concentrate on anything for long. She'd been sleeping badly and yet didn't feel tired; conversely she seemed to be filled with an inexplicable, nervous, restless energy.

But wasn't the explanation quite simple? Fern mused. No doubt she was worrying unconsciously as well as consciously about her and Carrie's futures. The strain of not knowing exactly what was going to happen when, or even if, Piers took over the estate was taking its toll. Probably David too was suffering from a similar anxiety.

Where was Piers? She been edgy, on tenterhooks for the last two days at work, expecting him to walk through the door at any moment. And, instead of being relieved when he'd failed to appear, she'd experienced a curious sense of deflation. Was this prolonged and mysterious absence simply another ploy to keep the pressure on David, or had Piers abandoned his claim to the estate and quietly returned to wherever he had come from?

'Are you all right, Aunt Fern?'

The childish voice jolted her back to the present. How long had Carrie been sitting there patiently with her knife and fork pushed together neatly on her empty plate? Quickly, Fern jumped to her feet and dished out the pudding into two plates, quietly amused that Carrie's relief that the apple sponge proved to be untainted was tinged with a certain amount of disappointment.

'Why don't you go and play in the garden while I wash up?' Fern carried the used plates over to the sink. 'Then we'll have a game of Snap before bedtime.'

Carrie nodded and then paused, hands thrust deep into the pockets of her cotton dungarees. 'I wish I was going to the Show with you tomorrow.'

Fern turned round, her heart constricting. 'I know, darling. But you'd soon get bored stuck in a tent with me all day. You'll have much more fun with Susie and her mummy and daddy.'

''Spose so,' Carrie sighed and picked up the stick that served as a pony from behind the back door, making clicking noises under her tongue as she vanished out into the garden.

Fern frowned. It was at times like this that the doubts assailed her. Had she made the right decision all those years ago in assuming responsibility for Carrie herself, rather than offering the baby up for adoption? Would it have been better for Carrie to have been brought up within a more conventional family unit? Fern's eyes softened as she glanced out of the window and watched the small figure charge across the lawn, guiding her 'pony' over huge imaginary fences. It was impossible to envisage a life without Carrie now.

The mundane chores completed, Fern hurried upstairs and exchanged her skirt and blouse for a faded pair of jeans and a dark green sweatshirt. Absently, she unpinned her hair, ran a comb through it, and then tied it back in a loose pony-tail, her attention directed outside. What was Carrie up to now? she wondered with amusement. The stick had been carefully tethered by the fence and the six-year-old was standing under the enormous oak tree that formed a boundary between the garden and the lane, evidently engaged in deep conversation with an overhanging branch.

'There's a kitten up there,' Carrie informed Fern a few moments later, as her aunt joined her.

Fern looked upwards and spotted the half-grown tabby cat crouched high on a branch, mewing raucously.

'I think it's stuck.' Carrie looked at her aunt with confident eyes.

Fern sighed resignedly, acknowledging the unspoken demand. 'C'mon, let's get the ladder.'

Hampered by Carrie's enthusiastic assistance, Fern eventually managed to manoeuvre the heavy, wooden ladder out into the lane and propped it up against the tree.

She climbed to the top rung and gingerly edged herself on to the branch alongside the tabby, making encouraging noises under her breath. The cat surveyed her with mysterious green eyes for a moment and then, with feline perverseness, casually began its descent.

'It's coming down on its own,' Carrie announced joyfully.

Fern sighed wryly, cautiously edging her way back to the ladder. Inadvertently she kicked it with her left foot and yelled out a warning to Carrie, as the ladder toppled backwards into the lane. Simultaneously, there was a squeal of brakes and a dull thud. Straddled securely across the branch, Fern peered down through the leaves and groaned in disbelief as she saw the familiar figure emerging from a blue saloon. The chances of anyone driving along the quiet lane at the precise second the ladder had fallen were a million to one . . . the chance of that person happening to be Piers Warrender . . .

'Aunt Fern's stuck up a tree.' Carrie's clear, piping voice carried distinctively in the still, evening air.

Fern cringed silently, her heart dropping as she saw the dark, mocking face looking up at her.

'So this is how you spend Friday evenings,' he drawled,

blue eyes brilliant.

'Only when there's nothing worth watching on the television,' she returned airily. 'Now would you mind fetching the ladder?' she demanded. 'Please,' she added unwillingly. For one awful moment she thought he was going to leave her stranded up here, but then he gave an infuriating deep chuckle and vanished from her line of vision.

'Thank you,' she muttered as she reached the ground safely, acknowledging Piers' steadying hand on the ladder. Automatically she glanced round for Carrie and saw her crouching by the hedge, unsuccessfully trying to entice the cat from its new haunt.

Fern's eyes were drawn back to Piers. Her hands felt damp and clammy, her legs curiously shaky. Anyone would have thought she'd run a marathon instead of merely climbing up and down a ladder!

'A little out of condition, aren't you?' Piers observed her flushed face lazily.

Fern froze, distrusting that gleam in his eyes. Surely he wasn't arrogant enough to think that her erratic breathing had anything to do with his unexpected appearance? She surveyed him coolly, taking in the well-worn jeans, navy shirt and the dark shadow around his jaw. 'Still not managed to find the key to your suitcase?' she murmured sympathetically. Her eyes flickered over his shoulder to the blue car, narrowing as she saw the large dent on the bonnet. Slowly, she moved across to the car, grimacing unconsciously as she studied the damage more closely. Ye gods, if Piers' reaction hadn't been so quick, the ladder would have landed on the open sun-roof. At the very least, Piers would have suffered a painful crack on the head.

She glanced back towards him. 'I'm sorry,' she murmured quietly.

He hadn't moved, but remained standing under the tree,

arms folded across his chest, watching her, his expression unreadable.

Fern frowned uncertainly. Why didn't he say something, yell at her . . . surely he must be furious about the car? His continuing silent appraisal unnerved her completely. She hated not knowing what was going on behind those shrouded blue eyes.

'Naturally, I shall pay for the repairs,' she continued formally.

He shrugged nonchalantly. 'I dare say the insurance covers low-flying ladders.'

There was a loud chortle from behind her and, startled, Fern spun round, her tension easing at the sight of Carrie standing a few feet away, her small face convulsed with laughter. Piers' facetious comment had evidently been heard and greatly appreciated by her.

Carrie's expression sobered and she took a step towards Piers, staring up at him with wide, serious grey eyes, sturdy small legs planted apart, her hands linked behind her back. 'We have hedgehogs in the garden sometimes,' she informed him earnestly.

Fern shot her niece a baffled glance. Now what on earth had prompted that remark? She was even more mystified when she saw Piers smile back down, evidently not in the least disconcerted by the strange confession.

'Would you like to see my nature table?'

'Carrie, I don't think——'Fern began gently, and paused dumbfounded as Piers' voice cut across her own.

'I'd like that very much,' he answered seriously, dropping to his haunches by the small girl.

Absently, Fern poured boiling milk into three mugs, listening to the sound of laughter echoing down the hall. How exactly had Piers engineered his way into the cottage? She was certain that she hadn't invited him. The whole situation seemed to have slipped out of her control.

Piers had inspected the nature table with a gravity and interest that had surprised Fern, having been convinced that he would make some flippant, banal comment, too insensitive to appreciate the honour that Carrie was bestowing upon him. Yet, instead, he had painstakingly identified the various feathers, cracked birds' eggs and sea shells that Carrie had studiously collected over the past months on expeditions into the Forest and to the coast. His knowledge, Fern grudgingly admitted, had been impressive as well as startling.

She placed the mugs on a tray. And now Piers was ensconced in the living-room, playing a boisterous game of Snap with Carrie. Fern picked up the tray and made her way along the narrow hall. Silky tendrils of hair had escaped from her pony-tail, framing her face, her cheeks were flushed, and her eyes dark with suppressed irritation. She resented the invidious position in which she was placed of having to treat Piers with a modicum of civility because of Carrie's presence. Her eyebrows drew together. The instant rapport that seemed to have sprung up between Carrie and Piers was another source of intense irritation. Carrie, normally reserved with strangers, was treating Piers like a much-favoured uncle.

She nudged open the living-room door and set the tray down on the table by the window, a shriek of delight from Carrie greeting her entrance.

'I've won,' she announced gleefully. 'You've got to be very quick,' she consoled Piers gently.

'I'm a little out of practice,' he murmured, the corners of the straight mouth twitching. He was sitting on the sofa, legs stretched out in front of him, while Carrie knelt by his side, an upturned cardboard box serving as a makeshift card table.

'Come and drink your cocoa at the table, please,' Fern

instructed her niece. 'And then it's bedtime.'

Carrie groaned out of principle but knew from past experience that there was little point in arguing.

Fern handed Piers his coffee, sitting down opposite him, relieved that Carrie's non-stop chatter kept his attention directed away from herself. She studied him through her lashes. He looked relaxed and comfortable, totally at ease with himself and his surroundings. He was so damn sure of himself, Fern thought with fierce resentment. Did he never doubt himself or his ability to deal with any situation in which he found himself? Did it never occur to him that his presence in her home was unwelcome?

'C'mon, Carrie.' She stood up abruptly, and Carrie reluctantly clambered down from her chair and bounded over to Piers to wish him a shy goodnight.

Fern paused in the doorway and glanced at Piers. 'I'll probably be quite a while,' she murmured crisply. 'Would you mind letting yourself out when you've finished your coffee?'

He quirked an eyebrow at her and deliberately stretched his arms high above his head. 'I'm in no hurry,' he drawled lazily.

'Why did you slam the door?' Carrie asked her aunt with deceptive innocence as she followed her up the stairs, thinking back to the number of times she had been reproved for a similar action.

'It slipped from my hand,' Fern muttered.

Bathed and clad in her pink and white pyjamas, Carrie snuggled down into her bed and looked up at Fern.

'I do like the hedgehog man,' she murmured confidingly.

Fern frowned. That was the second reference to hedgehogs that evening. Now why on earth should Piers remind Carrie of the prickly mammal? It was incomprehensible.

'Don't you think it's a little bit rude to call Mr Warrender the hedgehog man?' she asked gently. Hypocrite, she thought ruefully. Do as I say, not as I do!

Carrie's small face crinkled thoughtfully and then cleared. 'No,' she decided firmly. 'Because he is the hedgehog man. I saw him on the television. At Susie's. Yesterday. On that animal programme. He was talking about hedgehogs . . . and things,' she finished vaguely.

'Are you sure?' Fern asked doubtfully.

Carrie nodded vigorously and darted out of bed, padding over to her bookshelf. 'That's his.' She extracted a well-thumbed hardback and placed it carefully in Fern's hands. 'Honest,' she stated earnestly, sensing her aunt's scepticism.

Fern stared down at the book, one of Carrie's favourites. It was a simple, magical story about a dolphin, enchantingly illustrated with drawings and breathtaking photographs. The book was one in a series, most of which dealt with a member of a potentially endangered species, the aim of the author evidently being to educate future generations in the need for conservation. But the book's appeal, judging from the enormous worldwide sales, was not limited solely to children.

Slowly Fern turned the book over, already knowing what she would find. There was no revealing photograph, no potted biography; the only clue to the author's identity was the name Peter Wolfe, a pseudonym that had become synonymous in recent years with dramatic wildlife photographs. Was it possible . . . Piers Warrender, alias Peter Wolfe? No! It was too incredible to contemplate seriously for even a second. Carrie had made a mistake; the initials were pure coincidence.

Or were they? Fern brooded as she switched off Carrie's light and tiptoed from the room. She paused on the landing to draw the curtains. Carrie was a sensible, intelligent child, not given to wild flights of fancy. Uneasily, she recalled the surprising patience Piers had shown towards Carrie that evening, and patience was presumably an essential trait for a successful wildlife photographer. There was the well-informed interest he'd shown in the nature table . . . his absence over the past two days which, if Carrie was to be believed, would be explained by his attendance at a television studio in London. It all added up, Fern admitted unwillingly.

She opened the door of the living-room quietly. Piers hadn't moved, was still sprawled in exactly the same position as when she'd left. The room faced west and golden rays of the setting sun touched the dark hair, illuminated the harsh angles of the craggy face. He was so still that he could have been carved from granite, Fern thought suddenly. He never fidgeted, she registered; all his movements were controlled, purposeful, economical.

'Well, have I grown two heads?'

Fern flushed slightly, conscious of just how intense had been her scrutiny.

'I was just wondering what exactly you intend to do with Crofters,' she murmured coolly and distinctly, meeting his gaze squarely. 'Turn it into a nature reserve? How about a safari park? Think how convenient it would be to have all your subjects close at hand.' Somewhere in that deep blue she caught a glimpse of comprehension, all the confirmation she needed.

'Carrie?' he enquired laconically, raising a quizzical eyebrow.

She nodded, searching his face. 'Why didn't you tell me yourself?' she asked quietly.

'Is there any reason why I should have?' Ice-blue shutters dropped over his eyes. The lazy drawl had vanished, the deep voice cut through Fern like a razor. He had risen effortlessly to his feet and crossed the carpet with swift, silent steps so that he was barely a foot away from her. She wanted to step back, increase the space between herself and the lean, muscular frame, but forced herself to stand her ground. 'Would you have reacted any differently if you'd known?'

Fern gazed up into the harsh face, unable to equate the man who had earlier sat relaxed on the sofa, drinking coffee, gently teasing Carrie, with the cynical, remote stranger standing in front of her now. Did he really think that she was so shallow, so vacuous as to judge a man solely on his achievements and success? Was that what he was trying to imply? That she would have treated Peter Wolfe differently from Piers Warrender? The spark of anger ebbed as quickly as it had been ignited, to be replaced by a numbness and the shocked realisation that she minded very much that Piers should have formed such a low opinion of her.

'The telephone,' she muttered, overwhelmingly relieved that the shrill, demanding peal gave her a valid, dignified excuse for making an exit.

She returned a few moments later, her face troubled, Piers momentarily dismissed from her thoughts.

'Problems?'

'What?' she murmured vaguely, lulled by the sudden concern in the deep voice. 'Yes,' she admitted and sighed. 'Carrie was going to the Show with one of her schoolfriends tomorrow.' Why was she telling him all this? 'That was her mother on the phone. Apparently Susie's come down with the measles.' Thank goodness that was one hurdle she'd already overcome with Carrie.

'Why wasn't Carrie going with you?'

'I'm going to be too busy,' she started to explain. 'David needs me——'

'I see,' he cut through forcefully.

'And what exactly is that meant to mean?' she enquired heatedly.

He surveyed her with narrowed blue eyes. 'I was just

wondering how often Carrie is shunted off like an unwanted parcel because your fiancé needs you.'

'David is not . . .' She stopped, mouth compressed. She didn't have to offer Piers any explanations. If he wanted to think she neglected Carrie in any way, let him go ahead. The stress he had put on the world 'need' had been utterly distasteful. David was her employer—at least for the present—and she had no option other than to work tomorrow. Or did she? She wasn't compelled to do overtime. She could have refused, she now admitted uncomfortably, but she'd succumbed to that old weakness. And now it was too late to do anything about it. She couldn't let David down at the last minute.

'Goodnight,' she muttered, holding open the living-room door pointedly.

Piers remained where he was. 'And so what happens to Carrie now?'

'I hardly think that is any of your concern,' Fern murmured acidly, wanting to snub him as he had her.

'She can come with me,' he informed her calmly, hardly seeming to register that she had even spoken.

Fern stiffened. 'I shouldn't dream of imposing on you,' she said with icy politeness.

'*You* won't be,' he returned crisply, brushing by her as he moved out into the hall. 'I was inviting Carrie. She's a nice child, and there's no reason that she should miss out because——'

'She has a wicked aunt?' Fern scoffed. 'Oh, for heaven's sake, surely you can do better than that?' This was utterly ludicrous. Why were they arguing about Carrie, anyway? 'No wonder you write books for children,' she added to the departing back. 'You have the same mentality!'

'I'll be round to collect Carrie at nine,' he stated, slamming the front door closed behind him.

Fern leant against the hall wall and took a deep breath. He hadn't heard one word she'd said. Well, let him turn up in the morning if he wanted. But it would be a wasted journey, because she wasn't going to allow Carrie to go to the Show with him and that was final. She sighed, anger fading. The only loser in that case would be Carrie, she admitted reluctantly.

She wandered into the kitchen, made herself a much needed coffee and sat down on a stool, cupping her hands around the steaming mug. She felt confused, uncertain, drained and inexplicably depressed.

Her eyes clouded pensively. When she'd learned the truth about Piers' identity, surely her reaction should have been one of amazement, astonishment . . . yet instead she'd only been conscious of that knotted, twisted feeling in the pit of her stomach. It was identical to the feeling she'd experienced earlier in the evening when Piers had appeared out of the blue, offering no explanation at all for his absence. And she had been forced to accept that she had no right to expect or demand one.

Fern put her mug on the table and rested her chin in her hands, staring down into her coffee. She wished that Piers had told her himself that he was Peter Wolfe, hadn't let her discover it second-hand through Carrie. But then, her relationship with him so far had hardly been conducive to the exchanging of confidences, she reminded herself. She chewed her bottom lip. Somehow common sense and cool logic still didn't seem to ease that ache inside of her, the feeling of emptiness. It would appear, she acknowledged unhappily, that she wasn't quite as immune to Piers Warrender as she professed to be. And that was a terrifying admission.

Fern collected the registration fee from the serious-faced

teenage girl clad in immaculate cream jodhpurs and navy blue riding jacket, and handed her a number. 'The working-pony class starts at half-past one.' Briefly, she consulted the schedule lying open in front of her. 'In ring number four.'

The girl nodded and departed from the tent and, concealing a sigh, Fern turned her attention back to the red-faced man who had already monopolised her time for the past quarter of an hour, complaining bitterly about the standard of judging in one of the dog classes. Fortunately he didn't seem to require any response from her, so Fern simply listened patiently while he aired his grievances.

She'd had a succession of competitors filing through the tent all morning, registering their late entries in a diversity of events, ranging from equine and cattle classes to the children's pet show. For some the annual show was a deadly serious occasion, the culmination of a year's hard work, the rivalry between many of the local farmers exhibiting their prize livestock good-natured but intense; for others it was simply an enjoyable day out for the whole family, a chance to show off a beloved mongrel in one of the fun events—the dog or bitch with the waggiest tail, the one who most resembled its owner in appearance.

The red-faced man finally departed, muttering threats against persons unknown under his breath and headed for the beer tent.

Fern stood up from behind the trestle table and stretched her legs gratefully. The tent was stifling and she was longing for a drink. She should have come armed with a flask of cold orange juice, but her priority that morning had been getting an over-excited Carrie calmed down and ready in time for Piers' arrival.

She walked over to the entrance of the tent, her eyes wandering over to the throng of people packed into the showground, competitors looking hot in their thick breeches and jackets, mingling with the more scantily attired spectators, in a swirling mass of bodies.

Somewhere out there was Carrie. And Piers. Fern grinned self-consciously, remembering her panic of the previous night that had been dismissed in the clear light of day as absurd. She was prepared to admit that she was finding it increasingly difficult to completely ignore Piers' blatant, vital maleness, but she was certain she could govern her wilful hormones. On an emotional level, she assured herself confidently, she had nothing to fear at all.

She smiled as she saw the efficient-looking grey-haired woman approaching, recognising her as a member of the Show Committee of which David was chairman.

'I've come to relieve you for a while,' she told Fern briskly. 'Give you a chance to grab some lunch and have a wander around the grounds.'

'Thanks very much,' Fern murmured gratefully, following her back into the tent to retrieve her leather handbag.

'You look very charming today, my dear. That colour certainly suits you. And you should wear your hair like that much more often.'

Fern acknowledged the compliment with a faintly embarrassed smile, suddenly very conscious of the heavy mane of hair tumbling down her back. That morning, for the first time in a very long while, she'd had the urge to wear something pretty and bright, totally removed from her usual rather dreary, staid outfits. Without much hope, she had rummaged through her wardrobe and discovered the forgotten pale yellow sun-dress. She'd bought it several years ago, but the simple cotton sheath-style dress was dateless, and still fitted her perfectly. Her austere hairstyle had looked totally incongruous with the casual dress, so she had left it loose, smoothing it away from her face with two slides borrowed from Carrie.

Fern slung her handbag over a bare shoulder. 'I won't be too long,' she assured the older woman.

'Take your time, my dear. I'll be glad to sit down for a while!' She extracted a card from her skirt pocket. 'Could you give this to David on your way? It's the results of the Novice Jumping.'

'Of course.' Fern picked up the card and left the tent, heading for the commentary van situated by the main ring. As she neared it, she could hear David's voice coming over the tannoy, describing the heavy horses currently parading around the ring. Fern paused for a moment to watch the magnificent animals in their gleaming leather and brass harnesses—the chestnut Suffolks, the Percherons with their deep, compact bodies and immense hind quarters, the Clydesdales, and her own personal favourites, the huge, white-legged, gentle Shires. Suddenly Fern felt quite extraordinarily happy. There was no logical cause for the surge of well-being, other than the fact that the sun was warm on her bare shoulders and she'd escaped from the tent. But then, she mused with a wry smile, her moods seemed to be so transient anyway these past few days, changing swiftly from minute to minute for no rational reason.

She opened the door of the van and placed the card in front of David, who indicated with sign-language that he wanted her to wait for a moment. He covered the microphone with his hand.

'You're still coming to the party tonight, aren't you?'

'I'm not sure,' Fern answered evasively. She had originally planned to attend the party always held after the Show each year, and had accordingly arranged for Carrie to spend the night with the woman who minded her each day after school, but that had been before she'd broken off her engagement to David.

'Only I'd be very grateful if you'd act as my hostess tonight,' he said stiffly.

Fern shot him a puzzled glance. That was a role normally reserved for Annette Warrender.

'Mother has a migraine,' he explained. 'I doubt whether she'll be fit by this evening.'

'I am sorry,' Fern said dutifully. She hadn't been aware that Annette was prone to that particular misery, but then the poor woman was probably worried to death that she might lose her home. She had never much liked David's mother, but it was impossible not to feel sorry for her in the circumstances.

Her eyes flickered to David's white, drawn face. He was beginning to look really ill. How could Piers torture him and Annette like this? she thought fiercely. He was a successful and presumably wealthy man in his own right. He didn't need Crofters as well. How was he going to pursue his career, which necessitated travelling all over the world, and run the estate anyway?

'Of course I'll help out in any way I can,' she assured David gently. She owed him that much at least.

'Thanks,' he murmured, and she saw the dubious expression on his face as he surveyed the sun-dress. 'You will wear something suitable?'

'I've mislaid my grass skirt,' she answered drily.

Heaven help them if David ever had any daughters, she mused as she walked away from the van—they'd probably be shrouded from head to foot. She stopped at a kiosk and bought a cold mineral, drinking it thirstily. How strange that two men could share the same father and have such completely contrasting characters. She frowned, absently tossing her empty cup into a bin. But the fact that Piers had so little in common with his half-brother did not justify his callousness towards him.

Did David have any idea of Piers' identity? Well, she certainly was not going to enlighten him; it would only be rubbing yet more salt into the wound. It was rather surprising that Piers had managed to keep such a low profile over the years, she decided thoughtfully. But that state of affairs would doubtless change if he planned to make many more television appearances.

She drifted into the rare breeds exhibition area, studied the assortment of cattle and sheep, and then made her way to the display organised by the local Naturalists Society. Both would presumably be of interest to Piers—not that she was searching for *him,* of course, she reminded herself briskly, but for his small companion.

She glanced at her watch and decided reluctantly that she ought to be returning to the tent. She'd just have a quick look at the display of owls and birds of prey first. They were owned by a local girl who ran a programme of breeding barn owls and releasing them back into the wild.

As usual the stand was attracting a great deal of interest, but Fern managed to ease her way to the barrier that separated the birds from their admiring audience. She stared in fascination at the large European eagle owl with its large, mesmerising orange eyes, and then her whole body tensed as she saw the tall, dark-haired man engrossed in conversation with an attractive redhead in her late twenties, a buzzard perched on her well-protected outstretched arm. Beside them was Carrie, gazing up earnestly at the bird of prey.

As Piers smiled down into the young woman's eyes, Fern jerked her head away, spun round abruptly and tried to make her way back through the surging crowd, not analysing the reason for her haste, just knowing that the last thing in the world she wanted at that precise moment was for Piers to see her.

But it was too late to escape. Carrie had spotted her, and

was waving madly from behind the barrier. There was no alternative other than to retrace her steps.

CHAPTER FOUR

'WHAT are you doing here?' Fern asked her niece brightly as she slipped under the barrier to join her.

'Helping Piers and Sally with the owls,' Carrie informed her importantly.

'I see,' Fern smiled vaguely, uncomfortably aware of the woman standing possessively close to Piers, studying her with speculative, catlike green eyes.

'I patted one of those great big horses. And I've had two ice creams,' Carrie continued blithely, dispelling Fern's anxiety that the six-year-old might be getting tired and fractious by now. Carrie was evidently having a wonderful time with Piers—and Sally, Fern added to herself caustically.

'Do you know Sally Thornton?' Piers drawled.

'Only by sight,' Fern murmured politely as Piers made the brief introductions. That stiff little smile was beginning to make her jaw ache. 'Of course I've read your articles about barn owls in the local paper,' she added. Oh, heavens, she sounded just like Annette Warrender at her effusive worst. Why did she feel so tense and awkward? Even her voice sounded high and unnatural.

Sally was even more attractive seen at close quarters, with her clear, creamy skin, high cheekbones and golden red curls. There was more than a hint of sensuality in her full red lips, a promise that surely most men would find difficult to ignore. Automatically, Fern flicked a glance up at Piers and was disconcerted to realise that he was watching her with lazy blue eyes. Quite deliberately, his gaze dropped from her flushed face and lingered on her smooth, bare shoulders, the

73

flicker in his eyes disturbing. What had ever prompted her to wear the sun-dress? It was totally unsuitable for an agricultural show. She suddenly wished desperately that she was dressed in jeans and T-shirt like Sally. Except, she admitted, she would never have managed to look as elegant as the other girl in the casual wear.

She started, taking a hasty step backwards as the buzzard, still perched on Sally's arm, stretched its wings.

'King won't hurt you,' Sally assured her in an amused voice. 'He's perfectly tame. Why don't you stroke him?' There was an open challenge in the green eyes that Fern pretended not to see.

'No, thanks,' she murmured, eyeing the buzzard dubiously. She tried to smile airily, but didn't find it particularly amusing to be standing there with everyone grinning at her. Even Carrie, the little traitor, seemed to find her reluctance to go anywhere near the evil-eyed bird of prey hilarious.

'I must be getting back,' she murmured stiffly. She suddenly felt like an outsider, excluded by the easy familiarity that appeared to exist between Sally and Piers. It had never occurred to her that Piers might have friends in the area . . . especially women friends.

'See you later,' she murmured vaguely to no one in particular, and moved towards the barrier, pausing as she heard Piers' drawling voice behind her.

'Have you any objections if I take Carrie over to Sally's to see the other owls? Sally's going back to the sanctuary shortly, as it's so hot.'

'Of course not,' Fern lied brightly. She had plenty of objections, she realised uneasily, but they all seemed to relate to Sally. And that mood of well-being had well and truly vanished.

* * *

Fern stood with an untouched glass of wine in her hand, watching David dance energetically with a tall, dark-haired girl. He would appear to have forgotten his problems for the night—and her along with them. She smiled wryly and took a sip from her glass. At least her formal duties as hostess were over. The party was in full swing, people sauntering in and out of the marquee to replenish their plates and glasses from the lavish buffet and bar, talking in groups with loud, strident voices, dancing on the lawn that was illuminated with coloured fairy lights.

Unconsciously, Fern moved into the shadows on the edge of the lawn and stood under an old beech tree. She felt curiously isolated from the scene around her, unaffected by the music and laughter echoing in the tranquil night. In fact, she admitted honestly, she felt quite appallingly lonely. David would hardly miss her now, she decided, the thought of returning to the cottage enticing. At least she could take off her shoes and be lonely in comfort.

She hadn't left the showground until well after five, and it had been a mad scramble to arrive at Crofters in time to greet the first of the party guests. While Carrie had eaten her tea, she'd snatched a quick shower and changed into the long-sleeved grey dress with the silver belt, leaving her hair loose, not having the time or inclination to arrange it into a more elaborate style. She'd dropped Carrie off in the village and then driven the five miles back to Crofters. And all she longed to do now was go home and sit down on her comfortable sofa with her feet up.

She would slip through the trees and make her way discreetly round to the front of the house, she decided, having no desire to make her exit too public. She swallowed the rest of her wine and turned round, the glass slipping from her hand as, gasping with shock, she cannoned straight into a hard male form. Automatically her hands went out to steady herself and clutched a pair of broad, muscular shoulders.

'Piers!' she choked. 'What the hell do you think you're doing creeping around in the dark?' she demanded, anger replacing the momentary alarm.

'Waiting to fall into the arms of unsuspecting females,' he drawled, and she flushed, snatching her hands from his shoulders as if they had been scalded.

He gave a low chuckle, stooped down to retrieve the glass and handed it to her with mocking politeness. 'Yours, I believe.'

'Thanks,' she muttered ungraciously, and drew in her breath sharply as he emerged from the shadows. He was dressed in dark, slim-fitting trousers, expertly tailored to the lean hips and long, powerful legs, and a blue silk shirt. It was the first time she'd seen him wearing anything but jeans, and if it were possible he looked even more devastating, she admitted with a painful thud of her heart.

She swallowed, conscious of his eyes on her face. 'Thank you for taking Carrie today. She had a wonderful time,' she croaked, somewhat incongruously, searching desperately for a safe topic of conversation, his silent appraisal unnerving her completely.

'So did I,' he drawled. He turned his head, watching a group of dancers, and Fern flicked an undetected glance at his rugged profile.

Did his 'wonderful time' have anything to do with Sally Thornton?

'It was kind of Sally to show Carrie all the owls,' she said brightly. 'I was expecting to see her tonight,' she added nonchalantly. Sally had been in the car when Piers had dropped Carrie off at the cottage earlier that evening, and Fern had assumed that if Piers did make an appearance at the party tonight Sally would be at his side. She frowned. Had that had anything to do with her reluctance to come to the party herself? she wondered uneasily, knowing that if it hadn't been for her promise to David she would have avoided it completely.

'Unfortunately Sally couldn't make it tonight.'

'What a shame,' she murmured politely, knowing that she was simply paying lip-service to the words, wasn't sorry at all. 'Have you known her long?' she asked with studied casualness.

'I was at school with her brother,' Piers drawled. 'We've kept in touch over the years, usually meet up in London whenever I'm there.'

Was he referring to the brother or Sally? Then the remainder of his words registered.

'This isn't the first time you've been back to England?' she asked, staring at him with bewildered eyes. Why hadn't he been back to Crofters, at least for a visit, before now?

'No.' There was a finality to the word. She could see the muscles in his jaw tighten, an indication that this particular conversation was terminated, that any further questions about his personal life would not be tolerated.

Irritated, Fern turned her attention to the dancers that seemed to be occupying him, trying to block out his presence by her side. She couldn't help smiling as she saw David, arms wrapped round the dark-haired girl, as they danced languidly in time to the slow music. She was pleased to discover that not even her pride was wounded that he had found consolation so quickly. In fact, she was relieved, and glad that at least for tonight he appeared to be happy, the lines of strain temporarily erased from his face.

'Your fiancé seems to have abandoned you in favour of a younger model.'

'We're no longer engaged.' Fern immediately regretted the admission but his sneering comment had stung her.

'I see.' Blue eyes studied her speculatively. 'Well, in that case he can have no objections if I ask you to dance.'

She doubted whether Piers would care if David objected or not. She eyed him warily. She had anticipated some cynical remark at her expense and instead he was calmly inviting her to dance.

'I take it you can dance?' he drawled as she hesitated in answering.

'I even know how to use a knife and fork,' she snapped. Why did this man nettle her so much?

'Shall we, then?'

Expecting to see the familiar mockery on his face, she was taken aback by the intentness in his eyes. She wanted to refuse the invitation, but that would be admitting to the curling fear in the pit of her stomach at the thought of the inevitable intimacy involved in dancing together.

'Why not?' she answered lightly, placing her glass on the ground. She took a step forward, intending to join the swirl of dancers on the main lawn, and stiffened as Piers grasped her shoulders lightly and swung her round in front of him. His hand moved down to the curve of her waist, directing her movements to match his.

'Aren't we going to join the others?' Fern forced the words out. The warmth in the strong fingers clasping her hand made her throat constrict painfully.

'There's more room here.' His mouth was tantalisingly close to her right ear, his breath warm on her cheek.

Fern fixed her gaze at a point above his left shoulder to avoid looking directly into his face, but it was impossible not to be aware of his square jawline and uncompromising chin on a level with her forehead. She didn't want to dance out here under the stars alone with Piers. She hadn't bargained for this. His hand tightened on her waist, drawing her closer against the hard male form. She could feel the warmth of his body through the thin silk shirt; her sense of smell was assailed by the tang of male after-shave.

She tried to concentrate on the music, but all her senses seemed to be dominated by Piers. She didn't seem to be able to even breathe properly any more.

Dimly she was aware that they had come to a standstill, was conscious of the pressure of Piers' hand in the small of her back, moulding her body into his. Transfixed, she looked up at him, fighting the impulse to stretch up a hand and trace the line of that decisive jaw, and read the disturbing message in the dark blue eyes that were fixed steadily upon her mouth.

'I'd like another drink, please,' she choked desperately. For one heart-stopping moment she thought he was going to ignore her urgent plea, but then his hold lessened and his arms fell to his side. She could see a nerve pulsating at the base of his throat.

'Wine?' His voice sounded hoarse.

'Yes, please.' Her own voice was unsteady too.

She watched him walk away in the direction of the marquee, covering the ground with his loping strides. And then she turned away.

Fern stood under the shower, the cool water soothing her heated skin but having no calming effect on her agitated thoughts. That ruse of asking Piers for a drink, enabling her to escape during his absence, had been cowardly, ill-mannered and juvenile. But she'd been driven by churning panic, sparked by the terrifying knowledge of how little control she had over her physical response to a man she hardly knew, a man she didn't even like. And to think that she'd seriously considered she might be frigid, immune to physical attraction.

She turned off the shower, wrapped a towel around herself and padded across the landing to her bedroom. It had been a culmination of the soft music and unaccustomed wine going to her head that had made her behave so uncharacteristically, she reasoned. She sat down on her bed and groaned. Why did she keep persisting in this self-deception? It was Piers who had gone straight to her head! In only five days, he had managed to turn her whole world upside-down, had invaded her thoughts, made her feel emotions she never wanted to experience again.

Perhaps she should have guessed that Piers wouldn't simply ignore her departure, should have anticipated the sound of the doorbell, but she hadn't. She didn't move from the bed, listening to the insistent peal echoing through the small cottage. Surely he would go home eventually if she failed to respond to his summons? Her eyes darkened. Hiding wasn't going to solve any problems. It would be better to face Piers now, rather than spend a restless night, dreading their next encounter.

Quickly, she tugged on a pair of jeans and slipped a T-shirt over her head. Then, conscious of her braless state, she added a camouflaging sweater. She flicked her hair back over her shoulder, took a deep, controlling breath and walked slowly down the stairs.

The hall light spilled out into the porch illuminating the tall, familiar figure.

'Your drink,' Piers greeted her idly, holding out a glass.

His casualness threw her completely, made her forget her resolve to be brisk and dismissive. He was acting as if it was the most natural thing in the world to be standing on a porch in the middle of the night, proffering wine. Perhaps it was, for him!

'Sudden emergency?' he drawled, quirking an eyebrow. 'Nothing too serious, I hope.'

'Er—no. Thank you.' She eyed him warily. What was he playing at?

'May I come in, then?'

'I was just going to bed——'

'Dressed like that?' He surveyed the jeans and sweater. 'Even for you, isn't that carrying maidenly modesty a bit too far?'

He took a step towards her, towering over her. 'And now,' he demanded tersely, 'perhaps you'd like to tell me exactly why you did leave so abruptly.'

She tilted her head, looking at him squarely in the face, determined to ignore those alarming blue shadows in his eyes that threatened to induce the cramping fear again.

'Hasn't it occurred to you that I left simply because I was bored?'

She saw the dark eyebrows knit together.

'What's the matter?' she taunted. 'Have I bruised your male ego? Hasn't anyone ever walked out on you . . . Piers!' She winced as his fingers clamped around her upper arm, pulling her relentlessly towards him. His other hand curved around the back of her head, his fingers sliding through her hair, holding her immobile.

'Let me . . .'

His lips brushed her forehead, moved slowly over her closed eyes and along her cheekbones. The muscles in her body tautened, her mind battled to deny the slow, sensuous pleasure seducing her raw nerve-endings. She felt her resistance slipping away, and she was submerged in a warm bath of tantalising delight. His tongue traced the contour of her ear, left a scorching trail down her arched neck. The longing to feel that teasing, warm mouth on hers became a physical pain.

'Still bored?'

From a long way away, she heard the mocking voice and opened her eyes dazedly.

It was like walking out of a sauna into an icy shower as she saw the cool satisfaction in his eyes. Oh, he had proved his point, she thought with searing resentment, her fingers tightening on the glass, miraculously still intact in her left hand. She only intended to tip the wine over his shirt, but the glass slipped from her grasp, hitting the side of his face before crashing to the tiled floor and disintegrating into tiny pieces.

'You little bitch,' his voice lashed her.

She flinched from the anger in his eyes. 'I'm sorry,' she faltered.

'I'm sure you are,' he grated ominously, and then his mouth came down on hers in a punishing, merciless onslaught. There was no slow rise of warmth this time, just a scorching fire raging through her veins, making her dizzy and weak. She could feel her heart thudding against her ribcage. She could hardly breathe, his mouth grinding her lips against her teeth that were clenched together in a desperate attempt to repel a deeper, unwanted intimacy.

She was powerless in his arms, her breasts crushed against the hard wall of his chest. Then suddenly she felt the anger easing from his body, a different, even more frightening emotion taking its place. She could feel the hardening arousal of his body against her slender thighs, was aware, too, that she was no longer fighting him but kissing him back, responding to that fierce need inside her that made her forget everything but this man.

Fern's arms locked around Piers' neck as he carried her effortlessly into the lounge, bathed by the soft light of a single lamp, and stood her upright on the carpet. He gazed down at her with eyes that didn't seem to focus properly, his breathing ragged.

'Tell me to go,' he muttered hoarsely.

She tried to force the words through her parted lips, but nothing happened. And then it was too late anyway, as his mouth claimed hers again, probing the inner moistness between her pliant lips. His hands cupped the swelling breasts, his thumbs tracing the outline of the hardening nipples through the cumbersome clothing that was becoming a hindrance to them both. Fern offered no resistance as he pulled the sweater and T-shirt over her head in a swift, urgent movement, gasping with delighted shock as she felt his hands on her bare, heated skin. He dropped to one knee, his mouth taking the place of his hands. Fern arched her back, her fingers curling into the thick, dark hair as his tongue flicked teasingly over the throbbing, aching peaks.

As he rose to his feet, she swayed against him, her hands awkward and uncertain as they unbuttoned his shirt and began their first tentative exploration. She shuddered at the feel of the hard male skin beneath her palms, moving against him, the tips of her breasts brushing the hard wall of his roughened chest. With a deep groan, his mouth fastened on hers, drawing her down on to the carpet beside him. She heard the zip of her jeans slide down and raised her hips, helping him to ease the denims down over her long legs. There was a rustle of movement as Piers' clothes joined hers, and Fern's throat went dry at his male beauty, her eyes travelling over the wide, powerful shoulders, the flat stomach, the strong, muscular thighs. He lay on his side next to her and, with hands that grew in confidence, she discovered the hard, taut lines of his body, closing her mouth on the warm male flesh, wanting to pleasure him as he had her.

His breathing became more erratic, his knee moved between her legs, pushing them gently apart. As Fern felt the weight of his body lowering between her thighs, she stiffened, doused in icy waves of fear and panic. What was she doing here with this man? How had she ever let this happen, allowed her body to betray her mind?

'No!' she cried out despairingly, trying to push him away.

'It's all right, sweetheart. Just relax,' he whispered hoarsely, covering her face with small, heated kisses. Expert fingers caressed her, moved knowingly down the length of her silken body, arousing her to fever pitch. Instinctively, she started moving restlessly against him, arching her hips to meet the urgent demands of his body as he possessed her. Nerve-tingling sensations racked her body as he guided her to a pleasure so intense that she thought she was going to die. Her hands clasped his shoulders, her nails digging into his skin as she reached fulfilment, feeling Piers shudder against her, his voice hoarse against her throat.

Fern lay still in a languid haze of well-being as her breathing returned to normal, her fingers stroking the back of the dark head pressed against her breast. If only, she thought dreamily, she could stay like this forever. Then, as Piers stirred, the shock of what had just happened, what she had wanted to happen, hit her.

'Fern?' Piers eased himself on to his elbows, looking down at her. 'Do you always cry after you've made love?' he asked gently, smoothing back the damp tendrils of hair from her forehead.

She hadn't even been aware that she was crying until she tasted the salty tears running down her cheeks. She averted her head, rubbing the back of her hand across her eyes. She didn't even know what had caused the tears, unless it had something to do with that aching void inside of her, the contrast between those moments of soaring happiness and her present desolation.

She stiffened as Piers lifted a hand to cup her breast in a gesture of total familiarity that sent waves of shame flooding over her. She wanted to scream at him not to touch her, but fought desperately against the surging hysteria that threatened to engulf her completely. If she gave way to it now she knew she would start yelling wild accusations at him. Accusations that were unjustified and would merely make her look foolish and hopelessly naïve. She hadn't exactly been an unwilling victim—the red weals on his shoulders where her nails had scored his skin were a humiliating testimony to that. Nor had Piers deceived her in any way. Not even at the most intense moments of their lovemaking had he said anything that led her to suppose it was little more than just another enjoyable physical experience for him. Somehow she had to keep her emotions in check, had to pretend to treat this situation with the same casual indifference as Piers. She had suffered enough humiliation already without adding to it by causing a huge dramatic scene.

Yet even now, she didn't seem to have any control over her traitorous body, her skin quivering under Piers' caresses as his hand moved slowly downwards.

'No!' She couldn't stop her protest this time, pushing his hand violently away from her.

His eyes darkened. 'You don't like that?'

'I . . . you're hurting me. You're too heavy,' she lied hoarsely, desperate to be released from his imprisoning body.

'I'm sorry.' He moved off her, frowning with puzzlement as she immediately sat up and reached for her clothes, the need to cover her nakedness paramount.

'What are you doing?' he demanded, watching her with narrowed eyes.

'I should have thought that was obvious,' she returned coolly, keeping her back to him as she tugged the jeans over her hips.

He rose to his feet in a swift fluid movement, placed a hand on her shoulder and swung her round to face him. 'What the hell's the matter?'

Fern's throat constricted. Oh, God, she'd never realised a man could be so beautiful. It took every ounce of control to keep her eyes steady, her face expressionless. 'Nothing,' she said evenly. Except that she'd just undergone one of the most traumatic experiences of her life. 'Why should there be?' she murmured nonchalantly. Please get dressed and go home, she implored silently. She couldn't keep this act up much longer, and if she broke down now she would lose every last vestige of dignity. 'You're standing on my jumper,' she added pointedly.

She felt the pressure of his fingers increase on her shoulder, his eyes darkening until they appeared navy blue. Then wordlessly, he turned away, and started to retrieve his scattered clothing.

'Goodnight, Fern.'

She flicked him a wary glance as he moved towards the door. His face was a blank mask, his voice as unemotional as if he were taking his leave after a rather boring dinner party. Didn't he feel anything at all? It was impossible to imagine that so short a time ago they had lain in each other's arms, their bodies entwined together. She bit her lip to stop the swirl of hysterical laughter rising up inside her.

She nodded dismissively at him, not trusting herself to speak, and only when she heard the front door slam behind him did she start to laugh, the laughter swiftly giving way to scalding tears of anger and humiliation.

It would be so much easier if she could just hate Piers, she thought bitterly as she stood under the shower, soaping her skin ferociously in a desperate attempt to remove every trace of his male scent from her body. But right now she hated herself as well. Why had she ever opened the door to him in the first place, instead of listening to the warning bell clamouring in her head? Because, she reminded herself savagely, she hadn't realised quite how vulnerable loneliness had made her, hadn't anticipated that she would be so weak as to fall into his arms like some sexually frustrated widow. She cringed. Was that how Piers would view her easy submission? She felt so cheap . . . unclean. And that deep ache of loneliness hadn't been assuaged, merely aggravated.

Hadn't her marriage to Steven taught her anything? she wondered despairingly. Hadn't she learned to her cost how transitory was mere physical attraction, that sex without emotional commitment was unacceptable to her? Her face tightened. All the self-recriminations in the world weren't going to change anything. They wouldn't alleviate her shame, lessen her bitter regret. Her self-esteem had suffered a bad blow, but she'd recover, given time, she assured herself resolutely. Piers had possessed her body; he hadn't invaded her heart or her mind. The wounds were superficial and would heal. She grimaced. If only it were really that simple . . .

Fern woke feeling as if she'd spent the night in a sandstorm. Her eyes were smarting, her head ached and her throat was raw. But in some ways her physical discomfort was a blessing, for it anaesthetised her emotions. She felt too drained, too weary to think straight, and just concentrated on the simple tasks of getting dressed and making a swift cup of coffee before going to collect Carrie.

'Was Piers at the party last night?' Carrie demanded to know as they drove back towards the cottage.

'Yes.'

'Did you dance with him?'

'Mmm.' How could Carrie so unerringly choose the one topic she least wanted to discuss?

'Oh, good.' Carrie sighed with satisfaction. 'Do you like him? Better than David, anyway?'

This had gone quite far enough, Fern decided swiftly. 'Look, there's a rabbit on the verge. Quick, or you'll miss it,' she murmured, successfully diverting Carrie's attention away from herself.

She parked the car beside the cottage and followed Carrie

around to the front door, pausing in disbelief as she saw the huge floral bouquet lain in the porch.

'They're lovely,' Carrie buried her nose in the scented blooms before handing them to Fern. 'Who are they from?'

'I don't know,' Fern said shortly, opening the front door with her free hand, and then, feeling guilty at her brusqueness, added gently, 'There's no card.'

'It's a real mystery,' Carrie decided contentedly. 'Better put them in water,' she added sagely, and, losing interest, bounded up the stairs to her room.

Fern carried the flowers into the kitchen and tossed them on to the table with a scowl. Did it appeal to Piers' perverse sense of humour to send her an anonymous bouquet? For two pins she'd chuck them in the bin, except it seemed criminal to do that with such beautiful flowers. Besides, Carrie was sure to enquire after their whereabouts.

She jolted as the doorbell rang, trying to fight down the surge of illogical panic, and walked slowly out into the hall, throwing herself a quick glance in the mirror and grimacing at her reflection. She looked such a mess; her face was ashen, her eyes red-rimmed with huge, purple shadows underneath, and she hadn't even brushed her hair properly yet.

Taking a deep breath, she flung open the door.

'David!'

'Don't look so surprised. Who were you expecting?' the fair man greeted her. 'Did you find the flowers? They were by way of being a thank-you for helping out last night.'

'They're gorgeous,' Fern said quickly. She felt so foolish. How could she have ever supposed that . . .?

'I've just been down to the village and I saw your car was back, so I thought I'd just pop in and let you know that I won't be in the office until tomorrow afternoon.'

Fern nodded, studying him with puzzlement. He looked so happy and jubilant. And he had never given her flowers before, even while they were engaged.

'Piers is signing over the estate to me tomorrow.' He couldn't suppress the news any longer, grinning at Fern delightedly. 'We're going to the solicitors in the morning to finalise everything before Piers flies to New Zealand.'

CHAPTER FIVE

'THAT'S wonderful news,' Fern said brightly, wondering why she had to force the enthusiasm into her voice. Piers was flying back to New Zealand tomorrow. She would never have to see him again. She ought to be feeling relieved, overjoyed like David, and yet she just felt numb. Piers had never had any intention of taking over Crofters, she realised bitterly. It had all been a game to him, a game in which he had totally disregarded the feelings of those around him.

'Look, Fern, I know I've been rather tetchy lately.'

'You've been under a lot of pressure,' she answered automatically, and stiffened as he placed a hand on her shoulder.

'But now everything is back to normal,' he continued, looking deep into her eyes. He gave the boyish grin that never failed to irritate her. 'What I'm trying to say is that I want things to go back to the way they were between us. I was unreasonable the other day. But you were so wonderful as my hostess last night, I suddenly came to my senses and realised what a fool I'd been to let you go.'

Fern's heart dropped. An attempt at a reconciliation by David was the last thing she had expected or wanted. Was that why he had given her the flowers? Had he decided she might be suitable wife material after all?

'No, David,' she said flatly.

His smile evaporated and was replaced by the sulky expression she had always dreaded. 'Does this have anything to do with last night?'

She lowered her eyes, feeling sick. Surely Piers hadn't told

David . . . even he couldn't be that much of a swine . . .

'I only danced with the girl. I don't even know who she is,' David continued peevishly.

Fern started to breathe again. 'David, it's over,' she said gently. What had prompted all this? she wondered unhappily. She'd been naïve and over-optimistic, she realised, in believing that he had accepted the breaking off of their engagement with good grace. And why should he? she admitted honestly. She'd been unfair to him from the start.

'I see.' His face hardened and in that moment she could see the likeness between the two half-brothers. 'May I know the reason why?'

Why was he making it so difficult? she wondered despairingly. 'Because I don't love you,' she said evenly. She owed him the truth at least.

'There's someone else,' he accused her sharply.

'No,' she denied wearily. And there never would be. She'd married a man with whom she'd believed herself to be in love, and she'd been weak enough to become engaged to a man she didn't love. And both relationships had failed. She would never risk making a third disastrous mistake.

'It's going to be very difficult to go on working together,' David muttered after a lengthy pause.

Fern nodded, her stomach cramping as her worst fears were realised. Even worse was the knowledge that she had brought this on herself.

'You want me to hand in my notice?' she asked quietly.

'I think it would be best, don't you?'

'I'll stay until you find a replacement,' she answered steadily. Suddenly she felt as if she had been hit over the head with a sledgehammer. 'The cottage . . .' she tried to keep the desperation from her voice '. . . when would I have to leave the cottage?'

He shrugged. 'You'll have to discuss that with Piers.' He

elucidated as he saw her puzzlement, 'It's not part of the estate. It was left in trust for Piers by his mother.'

'What?' Fern exclaimed incredulously. No wonder Piers had seemed so surprised to find that she was living in Thyme Cottage. All this time he, not David, had been her landlord. Despair engulfed her. Even now, she thought drearily, she didn't seem to be free of Piers.

She waited until David had departed, then went back indoors and picked up the telephone, immediately replacing it again. This hesitancy was ridiculous, she admonished herself severely. She had to contact Piers before he left England and find out what he intended to do with the cottage. He might be planning to sell it, she thought unhappily. She bit her lip, staring down at the telephone. She was reluctant to speak to him and even more loath to have to call him at Sally Thornton's, where David had told her that Piers was spending his last day. And night? She pushed the thought from her mind and resolutely dialled the number with unsteady fingers.

'It's Fern Maynard,' she said with assumed briskness as she heard Sally's voice. 'May I speak to Piers, please?'

'I'm afraid he's rather busy at the moment,' Sally informed her coldly.

Fern gritted her teeth. 'It is rather urgent.'

There was a deep sigh. 'I suppose I'd better see if he'll speak to you, then.'

Fern kicked the hall table, grimacing as she stubbed her toe and then stiffened as she heard the familiar, deep voice in her ear.

'It's about Thyme Cottage,' she said, coming straight to the point, not bothering with even a cursory greeting. 'I was wondering if you'd consider letting it to me.' At a rent she could afford, she added silently.

'I'm sorry but it's out of the question. I have other plans

for the cottage.' There was no surprise or hesitancy in the terse voice. It was almost as if he had been anticipating her request. 'I intend to offer it to my secretary.'

'It's rather a long way for her to commute, isn't it?' she muttered caustically. Did he seriously expect her to believe that?

'What?'

She heard the bafflement in his voice and frowned uncertainly. 'To New Zealand every day,' she explained tentatively.

'Ah. I hate to disillusion you, but I'm only going to be in Auckland for a few days. I'm buying a house in the Forest.'

'You're going to live in England permanently?' she said weakly.

'Yes,' he drawled. 'Surely David can offer you alternative accommodation on the estate?' he added casually.

No doubt even Piers might balk at the prospect of having to evict her, she thought bitterly.

'I've—er—given in my notice,' she admitted reluctantly, and scowled as she heard the deep chuckle.

'You have been reckless, Mrs Maynard. No fiancé, no job and no fixed abode.'

She could see the dark, mocking face and gleaming blue eyes as clearly as if he had been standing right next to her. He was inhuman, she thought viciously. She had hardly expected sympathy from him, but that he could find her present predicament amusing . . .

'Of course, you could always work for me. Then you'd be able to stay in the cottage.'

'Work for you?' she echoed, stunned. Was he serious? 'You're the last . . .' She bit back her instinctive retort and took a deep, calming breath. It was a solution, she admitted uneasily, though hardly the one she would have chosen. She knew that she would have few problems finding another secretarial job in the area; the problem would be finding somewhere else to live. Most of the rented accommodation was let out to tourists at exorbitant rates she'd never be able to afford. Of course she could always move away from the New Forest, but that would entail uprooting Carrie yet again.

'Fern?'

'May I think about your offer?' She forced the words out reluctantly.

'I think you must have misunderstood me. I wasn't actually offering the position to you, merely suggesting that you might like to apply for it. Naturally I shall have other candidates to consider. Sorry, Fern, I didn't quite catch that?'

'Nothing,' she ground through clenched teeth.

'Right,' he said with a cheerfulness that made her want to scream. 'I'll let you know my decision either way in a couple of weeks.'

'But——' It was too late, he'd replaced the receiver. She hadn't definitely said she was even interested in the job, she thought ferociously. But then, she admitted, her anger ebbing. it was highly unlikely that Piers was going to employ her anyway.

Slowly, she wandered back down the hall towards the kitchen. At least he had made no reference to last night during their conversation, but then it would hardly have been diplomatic to do so with Sally within earshot. She frowned. The whole episode was beginning to assume a dream—or nightmare—quality now. It was as if the person who had made love with Piers had been someone else, not her at all. And right now, she reminded herself briskly, she had far more important matters to think about than Piers Warrender . . . like finding a new job and somewhere for her and Carrie to live.

Why did the weather have to break today of all days? Fern lamented as she pedalled furiously up the long, tree-lined drive, the sheeting rain lashing against her face. Breathlessly she rounded the last bend and caught her first glimpse of the secluded Georgian house, the purple and red brick giving an illusion of warmth and reflected sunlight under the grey, overcast sky.

To the west, pastureland ran down to a wide brook; on the other three sides the house was skirted by the open forest. Fern clambered off her bike and pushed it the last few yards, gazing up at the house. On a clear day the view from the dormer windows, set high up under the hipped tile roof, must be spectacular. Not that she was ever going to have a chance to find out, she thought ruefully. She very much doubted that the owner was going to give her a conducted tour of Avonbrook, however much she might have liked one.

She propped the bike against the side of the house and climbed the three wide steps to the impressive front door and heaved a sigh as she pressed the bell. Arriving like a drowned rat on the first day of a new job wasn't exactly the most auspicious of starts, she mused gloomily. She defied anyone to look brisk and efficient with water dripping down their neck and their hair plastered to their head like a skull cap.

The door was flung open.

'You're late!'

Three minutes, Fern acknowledged sourly, glowering at the tall figure. She was soaked to the skin, and all he could damn well say was that she was late.

'I suppose you're going to tell me that the car wouldn't start.'

'No. I have a fetish for cycling in the pouring rain,' she snapped back and turned on her heel.

'Where the hell are you going? You've only just arrived, for Pete's sake.'

'I'm going home,' Fern flung over her shoulder. It had all been a dreadful mistake. She must have been crazy to think even for a second that she would be able to work for Piers. She had only to look at him and something seemed to spark inside of her. How could she possibly spend eight hours a day cooped up in this house with him and remain sane?

'We agreed to a month's trial on either side,' he growled from the steps.

'Sue me for breach of contract,' she muttered, picking up her bike.

'Carrie must be looking forward to breaking up for the school holidays next month.'

She froze. How easily he had found her Achilles' heel. He might just as well have put a gun to her head and he knew it. She needed the cottage for Carrie and working for Piers was the price she had to pay. Defeatedly, she slung her bike down and, with hatred in her eyes, turned round.

'Action replay?' Piers quirked an eyebrow as she mounted the three steps again.

She ignored the remark and moved ahead of him into the large, tiled hall.

'I'd like to change,' she said curtly as he closed the front door. 'I've brought some dry clothes with me.' She indicated the waterproof bag clutched in her left hand. 'Don't worry,' she added caustically under her breath, 'I'll make up the time in my lunch-hour,' and then she froze as she felt his hands on her shoulders, eyes widening in alarm.

'I'll take your coat and hang it to dry,' he said brusquely.

'Oh, yes. Thanks,' she muttered awkwardly, slipping her arms from the coat, ashamed of that momentary panic.

'You can use the library to change in,' he continued, striding down the hall and opening a door on the left. 'Or the bathroom if you prefer. Upstairs, first on the right.'

'This will do,' she answered ungraciously, careful to avoid brushing against him as she passed by him into the large square room.

It was an infinitely masculine room, she decided as she stripped off her wet clothing and surveyed the deep, leather armchairs, book-lined walls and walnut desk. There were no ornaments, just one large water-colour above the fireplace. She zipped up her navy-blue skirt and tugged a matching cotton jumper over her head, and then frowned as her eyes rested on the new, flowery chintz curtains. They looked totally incongruous with the rest of the room. Somehow she couldn't imagine Piers having chosen them. Was he going to live in Avonbrook on his own, or did he plan to have a housekeeper? Or a wife? Her face tightened. Did Sally Thornton have anything to do with Piers' decision to settle in England? She shook her head, irritated with herself. This speculation was pointless. Piers' private life was of no concern—or interest—to her.

Flicking her hair back over her shoulders, she emerged from the library, and was taken aback to find Piers waiting for her in the hall, leaning against the curving banisters of the ornate staircase.

'Why did you feel it necessary to lock the library door?'

She was disconcerted by the unexpected abrupt question, confused by the icy glitter in his eyes.

'I . . . ' She shrugged, at a loss for words. She hadn't even been aware that she had locked the door behind her until he'd pointed it out. It had been an instinctive, totally unconscious action and she failed to understand what he was trying to imply.

'For the same reason you flinch every time I come anywhere near you?' he growled, and moved towards her. 'There you go again, jumping back like a scalded cat!' he thundered as she took an involuntary step backwards.

She stared up at him warily. She had never seen him so angry.

'I think we'd better get one thing straight right from the

beginning,' he continued harshly. 'What happened between us the night of the party was a mistake—and one I have no intention of repeating.'

The colour ebbed from Fern's face. This was the last thing she wanted to discuss.

'So you can stop recoiling like a terrified virgin every time I come anywhere near you!' His eyes raked her face. 'The only relationship I'm interested in is a working one. Otherwise I should hardly have employed you. I can assure you that I'm not in the habit of seducing my secretary.'

'I should hardly have accepted the job had I thought otherwise,' Fern said evenly, her controlled voice and impassive expression betraying nothing of her inner agitation. He'd made her sound so ridiculous. The trouble was, she hadn't known what to think when Piers had written to her a week ago and made her a job offer it was virtually impossible to refuse. Not only was she to remain in Thyme Cottage with a salary that was more than generous, but he'd also implied that she might occasionally be able to work from home during the school holidays. She'd been stunned and bewildered. Her skills were good, but she knew from the response to David's advertisement for her replacement that there were dozens of secretaries with far more experience than herself. So why hadn't Piers chosen one of them?

She looked up squarely into his face. 'Why *did* you offer the job to me?' she asked candidly.

For a moment she thought he wasn't going to answer. The anger had drained from his face, but he still looked cold and forbidding.

'You had the necessary personal attributes,' he said shortly.

She frowned, mystified.

'I'm a wildlife photographer,' he said quietly. 'I record what I see. I don't interfere with nature, which can sometimes appear to be very cruel.'

She nodded, uncertain as to where this was leading but intrigued nevertheless. She had often wondered when watching wildlife documentaries on the television whether the film crew were ever tempted to intervene as they filmed a predator attacking its weaker, vulnerable prey.

'I also undertake a certain amount of work for various conservation groups.' He paused for a moment, and shrugged resignedly. 'Some of the subjects I deal with are not very edifying.'

'Shock tactics,' Fern murmured understandingly. 'Nature's cruel, but man is even more so.'

'Exactly. So it is essential that whoever works for me isn't unduly sensitive or over-emotional, and thinks with their head and not their heart. I don't want a secretary who is going to burst into tears every time——'

'I see,' she cut in quickly, not wanting to hear any more, averting her face so that he wouldn't see the shooting pain in her eyes until she'd managed to control her expression. He made her sound as if she had as much feeling as a block of concrete. And even more distressing was the realisation that this man had the power to hurt her.

'And now perhaps we could start work?' he said drily.

Work was the operative word, Fern decided wryly at the end of her first week. She'd returned home to Thyme Cottage each evening, weary to the point of exhaustion. It wasn't that the job itself was unduly demanding, she recognised during her second week; it was the strain of being with Piers all day that was taking its toll on her energies.

She never seemed able to relax. Even when he left her alone in the light, airy morning-room that he'd adapted to serve as his office, she remained on tenterhooks, waiting for his return, trying to gauge his mood the moment he walked back through the door. It was his erratic moods that she found so nerve-racking and draining. Sometimes he would treat her with cool, almost exaggerated politeness, and then, for no apparent reason, he would become curt to the point of rudeness, barking orders at her, expecting an instant response to his demands. And that hadn't been easy in the first few days, before she'd had time to familiarise herself with the office layout. His filing system baffled her completely, seeming to defy all logic, but when she'd tentatively suggested that she might rearrange it he had snapped her head off. He also seemed to expect her to know by instinct to whom he would speak on the telephone, and to whom she had to invent an immediate excuse for his absence.

At other times he was morose and distant, hardly seeming to register that she was even in the room, not addressing her unless absolutely essential. Like yesterday, Fern thought sourly, glancing up from her typewriter to where Piers was sitting at the far end of the long room behind a large, rectangular table, strewn with papers. When he ran out of space on the table, the papers were spread around him on the carpet. She had been warned in no uncertain terms never to touch those papers, although secretly she ached to tidy them into neat piles.

He was working on a series of illustrated articles for one of the Sunday papers at present, but, judging from the way his waste-paper bin filled with screwed-up paper balls each day, it was not going very successfully. Surely he'd find it easier to concentrate in the study or the library, without the distraction of the typewriter, Fern mused. Or did he think she would down tools if he weren't there to oversee her?

She checked the letter she had just completed typing for errors and, satisfied, pulled it from the electric machine and placed it in her out-tray, along with the other letters Piers had dictated to her earlier that morning, to await his signature.

She glanced over to the bowed dark head again.

'I'm going for lunch now,' she announced bluntly. She'd quickly discovered that if she didn't stand her ground he would conveniently forget all about her hour's break, seeming to have no need of a respite himself.

He looked up and gave a slow, lazy grin. 'Is that the time already?'

'Yes,' Fern said shortly, her eyes darkening warily. It was these occasional flashes of good humour that she found the most disconcerting of all his moods. The sudden unexpected smile would catch her totally off guard, make her stomach muscles contract—the way they were doing now.

He stretched his hands high above his head. 'You know, as it's such a glorious day, I'm very tempted to join you outside for lunch,' he drawled idly.

Fern's expression froze. The last thing she wanted during her hour's reprieve was Piers' company. One of the chief reasons she went out into the garden, weather permitting, to eat her sandwiches was to escape from Piers!

'Actually, I was planning to do the weekend shopping today,' she lied quickly. It would save doing it tomorrow morning, she supposed.

'I see.' The lazy drawl had vanished from his voice. His eyes rested on her face and Fern had the uncomfortable sensation that he knew she'd just invented the excuse. He bent his head over his desk. 'Would you ask Mrs Roberts to bring me a sandwich and a coffee, please?' he said curtly without glancing up again.

'Yes.' She moved to the door, relieved that he had evidently decided to take a working lunch as usual.

Fern walked into the kitchen and relayed her message to the plump, motherly-looking woman who had materialised at the beginning of the week. She was driven up to the house each morning by her husband, who spent the day working in the garden.

'Did he say what sort of filling he wanted?' Mrs Roberts started to fuss.

'No.' Try arsenic.

'Salad,' the older woman decided comfortably after a moment's thought. 'And a couple of my special rock cakes. He was always partial to those as a boy. There's a cup of tea in the pot, love, if you want to help yourself,' she added.

'Thanks, Mrs Roberts.' Fern selected a mug from the wall cupboard and sat down at the huge refectory table with her tea, watching the older woman butter slices of bread. She'd skip the shopping after all, she decided, the thought of trudging around with a supermarket trolley singularly unappealing. Maybe she'd just go for a stroll after she'd eaten her sandwiches. She fished out her lunch box from her bag and then decided she didn't feel very hungry after all. In fact, the smell issuing from the oven, presumably the rock cakes, was making her feel slightly queasy. Suddenly she frowned, finally seeming to register all of Mrs Roberts' casual words.

'You knew Piers as a boy?'

'Oh, bless you, yes.' The plump woman moved across to the oven and extracted the cakes. 'I looked after him up at Crofters after his mother died. He was only three months old, poor little mite, and his father didn't know what to do with him.' Carefully, she placed the cakes on a cooling tray. 'Course, after he remarried, I thought I'd be given notice, but that Annette Warrender wasn't interested in looking after another woman's child, so I was asked to stay on. Which was a good job, I can tell you. After Annette had her own baby, she acted like Piers didn't even exist.' She paused in her monologue to place the sandwich and two warm rock cakes on a plate. 'That David was a sly little devil. Always up to mischief, but he'd never own up to it when it was found out, and Piers was always punished instead.' She sighed reminiscently. 'I'll just take this on through to him.'

Fern nodded, sipping her tea absently, trying to ignore that unexpected swell of compassion rising up within her. She didn't want to feel sympathy for Piers, not even for the boy he had been. She glanced up as Mrs Roberts returned, empty-handed.

'Fancy a rock cake yourself, love?'

'No, thanks,' Fern murmured, concealing her shudder. 'What was Piers like as a child?' she asked with studied casualness as the other woman joined her at the table with her own mug of tea. She didn't know what had prompted the question, or why it should be so important that she learn the answer. After all, it was human nature to be curious about one's employer, she convinced herself.

'Very even-tempered. Gentle, too. Just like his mother, God rest her soul.'

He'd evidently undergone a severe personality change over the years, Fern thought waspishly.

'Course he was always animal mad, even as a small child.' Mrs Roberts heaved a mournful sigh and shook her head. 'When he was older, he had some terrible arguments with his father, who couldn't understand why he wouldn't go hunting and shooting like David. He thought Piers was soft and a bit——' She made a gesture with her left hand.

'Effeminate?' Fern nearly choked. That was about the last adjective applicable to Piers Warrender!

Mrs Roberts nodded her confirmation. 'Just because he didn't want to go rushing around the countryside killing things.'

It was easy to see whose side Mrs Roberts had been on all those years ago, Fern smiled to herself. At least Piers had always had one ally. Strange that should suddenly matter so much.

'It took a lot of courage for Piers to stand up to his father the way he did,' Mrs Roberts said quietly after a reflective pause. 'James Warrender was a very hard man, and used to getting his own way.' She shrugged. 'Then one day Piers just walked out of the house and never came back. More tea?'

'Mmm. Thanks.' Fern wondered how Piers would react if he learned how exactly she had spent her lunch break! She ought not to be sitting here, gossiping about her employer, but . . .

'He used to send me postcards, from all over the world, so I always knew he was all right. I never told anyone else, though, not at first,' she admitted with a satisfied smile. 'Thought it would do them good to worry. Not that they ever did. Just seemed glad he had gone.'

And Annette must have thought that, with Piers' fortuitous disappearance, the estate would now inevitably pass to her own beloved son, Fern mused, gazing into her tea. James Warrender's will must have come as an awful shock to her; she must have been living in constant dread for the past five years that the wanderer would turn up. Which he had done. Fern frowned. Why on earth had James Warrender made such an extraordinary will in the first place?

'You could have knocked me down with a feather when he wrote to me three months back and said that he was coming back to live in England, and asked if me and my Bert wanted to work for him.'

So Piers had made his decision three months ago, Fern absorbed. It merely confirmed what she had earlier suspected, that Piers had never had any intention of claiming his inheritance. Crofters could hardly hold many happy memories for him. Perhaps, too, she could understand the temptation to taunt Annette and David for a while. But that didn't mean she condoned his action, she reminded herself forcefully. It had still been a cruel, callous thing to do.

'That woman's here again! That's the third time this week.'

Mrs Roberts' hiss broke through her straying thoughts and Fern looked up startled.

'Saw her go past the window.' Mrs Roberts' mouth tightened disapprovingly. 'The way she just walks in as if she owns the place . . .' She compressed her lips together as the back door opened and Sally Thornton walked through into the kitchen.

''Afternoon, Mrs Roberts. Fern.'

'Hello,' Fern murmured back without much enthusiasm, wondering why the sight of the vivacious redhead should always make her feel so depressed.

'Where's Piers? Office?'

Receiving a confirming nod from a dour-faced Mrs Roberts, Sally sauntered across the tiled floor to the door that led into the hall. 'Oh, Fern,' she called back over a slim shoulder, 'could you bring a cup of tea through to me? I'm simply gasping.'

There was a moment's silence in the kitchen as Sally vanished and Fern met Mrs Roberts' shrewd brown eyes and glimpsed a reflection of her own suppressed irritation.

'Expecting you to run around after her like that!'

Fern shrugged and stood up to fetch a cup and saucer from the cupboard. Her own strong antipathy to the other girl was something she didn't care to analyse. 'It's about time I was getting back anyway.'

'Don't you go letting him work you too hard, love. You're looking proper peaky today.'

'I'm fine,' Fern lied quickly, averting her face from the all too observant eyes. It had been a mistake to sit in the warm kitchen all this time. She should have gone for that walk outside that she'd promised herself.

She poured tea into the cup watched by a disapproving Mrs

Roberts.

'She can't seem to leave him alone for five minutes. Always phoning or just turning up.'

Fern didn't respond. Presumably Piers didn't want Sally to leave him alone.

'I'll tell you one thing. If he's crazy enough to marry her, I won't go on working here and that's a fact.'

Fern tried to smile as she picked up the cup and moved to the door, but her lips wouldn't seem to move.

Sally was standing by one of the large windows when Fern entered the morning-room-cum-office, fingering the russet velvet curtains.

'You simply must have some new ones,' she said to Piers, who had swivelled his chair around to face her.

'They look fine to me,' he muttered.

Fern glanced at his face. He didn't look exactly overjoyed to see Sally, she observed, and was immediately ashamed that the realisation should please her so much.

'What do you think?' He glanced around unexpectedly at her.

'I like them,' she stated firmly, surprised that he should have sought her opinion, and then had the sneaking suspicion that she would have approved the curtains even if they'd been lurid orange with scarlet stripes, just to contradict Sally.

A fleeting look of annoyance passed across the other girl's face and then she smiled down sweetly at Piers. 'Have you managed to look at those carpet samples I brought yesterday? Oh, Fern, would you put my tea down there?' she ordered, waving a vague hand in the direction of Piers' table.

Fern paused, and then gave way to temptation and placed the cup on the pile of papers.

'Not there, dammit!' Piers roared, leaping to his feet.

'Sorry,' Fern murmured innocently. They reached for the

offending cup together and it took Fern every ounce of control not to immediately snatch her hand away as it encountered strong, lean fingers instead of the expected china. In that second she was appalled to realise just how aware of Piers she was, appalled to discover that his slightest inadvertent touch could send those tingling shock-waves coursing through her.

Her face deliberately deadpan, betraying nothing of that brief agitation, she turned away and walked over to her own desk and started to flick through the in-tray. So Piers had finally managed to complete the first article, she mused, and started to copy it out.

She tried to shut Piers and Sally out, tried to concentrate on what she was doing, but it was hopeless. They were talking about the owl sanctuary now. Fern flicked them a glance from under her lashes. Sally had drawn up a chair close to Piers, her knees practically touching his. Fern scowled down at her desk.

Why couldn't Piers take Sally into another room? It made her feel so awkward, sitting here, trying to be unobtrusive. Her scowl deepened. If Sally did become the mistress of Avonbrook she would join Mrs Roberts in resigning. That was assuming she was still working for Piers by then, she reminded herself uneasily, her eyes clouding apprehensively.

'I'm sorry, I didn't quite catch all that,' Fern murmured absently, pencil poised above her shorthand book, as she glanced over to where Piers was standing by the open window, his habitual place when dictating.

'What the hell's the matter with you?' He ran an impatient hand through his dark hair. 'You've been in a daze all week,' he said tersely. 'You even turned up an hour late on Wednesday——'

'I phoned to say I was going to be late,' she interrupted

defensively. 'And I worked through my lunch-hour to make up the time.'

'You phoned and told me what exactly?' he demanded caustically. "Sorry, Piers, I'm going to be a bit late," he mimicked her voice unkindly. 'No excuse, no reason.'

Fern's face tightened and she stared down at her notebook.

'And you've been here precisely ten minutes this morning and you look half asleep.'

Sleep was something that had eluded her completely over the past week. Night after night, she had lain awake, staring up into the darkness, eventually falling into a fitful, restless doze before dawn, to be woken a short time later by the insistent clamouring of her alarm clock.

He moved across the carpet and sat down behind his desk, leaning back in his chair as he surveyed her with cool eyes.

'You realise that your month's trial is up today?'

'Yes,' she answered shortly. Was that some kind of threat? Pull up your socks or else? She sighed inwardly. What difference did it make in the end if he fired her or she left of her own accord? The outcome would be the same.

'Oh, go and make some coffee,' he ordered dismissively. 'Perhaps that will wake you up.'

She nodded, rising to her feet, and to her horror felt the familiar, gagging bitterness in her throat. Terrified of committing that ultimate humiliation, she clamped a hand over her mouth and rushed from the room.

She only just made it to the small cloakroom in time, and retched over and over again into the white basin. Her legs felt like lumps of jelly, her head was spinning like a child's top. Trembling, she clutched the sides of the basin, waiting for the nausea to pass.

Then it seemed to take every ounce of energy she possessed simply to turn on the cold-water tap and wash her face. Wishing she could just curl up in a dark corner and die, she emerged unsteadily from the cloakroom and saw Piers walking down the hall towards her.

He took one look at her ashen face and wordlessly propelled her into the library.

'Lie down,' he ordered, pushing her gently down on to the large leather sofa.

She wanted to protest, but it seemed so much easier just to do as she was told. She stretched her legs out, and leant back against a cushion, closing her eyes, willing her head to clear, hardly aware that Piers had left the room until he returned with a rug and placed it over her.

'Thanks,' she muttered, and slowly she began to stop shivering as the warmth crept back through her body.

'Feeling better?' he asked quietly. He was sitting opposite her in an armchair.

'Mmm.' She struggled upright and took a sip of water from the glass Piers had put by the sofa. She smiled wanly. 'It must have been——'

'Something you've eaten?' he broke in sardonically. 'How about a hangover?' His eyes were like ice. 'Shall we pass on the fairy-tales? You're pregnant, aren't you?' he said bluntly.

'I . . .' The words wouldn't form on her dry lips, but she knew that Piers would only have to look at her face to know the truth.

How could he have known? The question hammered in her head as she stared at him with wide, shocked eyes. Had it been a mere shot in the dark? How could he have guessed?

'I heard you being sick a couple of mornings last week,' he said matter-of-factly, as if reading her mind.

She couldn't take her eyes from his face, burning with embarrassed horror at his words, the rug now stifling her.

'I had my suspicions then,' he continued quietly. 'It seemed odd that you didn't even mention you were feeling unwell. Then, when you were "unavoidably detained" at home on

Wednesday,' he shrugged, 'and now this morning . . .'

'Quite the little Sherlock Holmes,' Fern said bitterly. He ignored her, rising abruptly to his feet and striding over to the window, staring out across the lawn. 'Have you told David yet?'

'David! Why should I?' She clenched her teeth together to stop that shrill, hysterical voice that must have been hers. Dear God, he thought . . .

He turned round slowly and his eyes raked her face. 'So I'm the father.' His voice was unemotional, controlled, but she could see a muscle flickering in his jaw.

'Yes,' she said quietly. She wanted to deny it but somehow that seemed to be a betrayal of the small human being inside of her. She couldn't lie to Piers, not about that.

'I should have been more careful,' he said quietly. 'Taken precautions. But I assumed that . . .'

'I was taking the Pill?' she choked, guessing immediately what he was implying.

He nodded. 'It was a natural assumption under the circumstances. You had been engaged to David for some time.'

She wanted to cry out her protest, tell him that, other than her husband, he was the only man with whom she'd ever made love. He thought she'd leapt out of David's bed into his—figuratively speaking. Unconsciously her fingers tore savagely at the fringe on the rug. And yet if he really did believe that, why was he so willing to accept that the baby was his?

'Were you going to tell me?' His voice sounded strained and unnatural.

'I don't know.' That was the truth. Her immediate reaction, when her growing suspicions had been finally confirmed by the result of her test on Saturday, had been to hand in her notice and move away from the district. To run away from

Piers, in fact, she admitted. Then slowly doubts had assailed her. Did she honestly want her child to grow up like Carrie, without knowing who her father was? Wasn't it the right of every child to at least know who had been responsible for its entry into the world?

'Didn't it occur to you that I might have some interest in the fact that you were carrying my child?'

'It's my problem,' she said evasively. How odd he looked and sounded.

'And how exactly are you planning to deal with this "problem"?'

She lowered her eyes. He sounded so cold and clinical now. It's not a problem, she wanted to scream at him. It's a baby. 'There are various alternatives.'

'Is abortion on the agenda?' his voice suddenly lashed at her.

Fern's eyes widened with shock and disgust, one hand reaching down across her abdomen as if to ward off an attack on the unborn child. 'No!' she choked. How could he even think that she would contemplate that course of action? She swallowed convulsively, fighting for composure. Feeling calmer, she raised her head and looked over to Piers. He had returned to his original position in the armchair and was studying her with enigmatic blue eyes. If only she really knew what was going on inside that dark head, Fern thought with sudden desperation.

'I'm going to keep the baby,' she finally admitted quietly.

'And how do you propose to support and look after Carrie and an infant? His eyes never strayed from her face.

'I'll manage.' Hadn't she been asking herself the same question a million times over? 'Single parents aren't exactly a rarity these days.' Other women coped in similar situations, she thought resolutely. And so would she.

'There is one obvious solution, of course.'

Her head jerked up. 'I don't want any help from you!' she said flatly. Could she really afford to be that proud? But the thought of Piers giving her money, paying her off, made her feel ill.

'Paying maintenance wasn't exactly what I had in mind——' He broke off in answer to the knock on the library door. 'Come in.'

Mrs Roberts walked in, her eyes avid with ill-concealed curiosity as she saw Fern lying on the sofa. 'Sorry to disturb you,' she murmured, not looking in the least apologetic. 'But the telephone in the office keeps ringing.' Mrs Roberts, Fern had discovered, did not consider answering the telephone to be one of her duties.

'Let it ring,' Piers said easily, and Fern stared at him warily as she saw the smile on his face. 'Mrs Roberts, I'd like you to be the first to hear the good news. Fern and I are getting married.'

CHAPTER SIX

FERN couldn't move; her whole body was rigid with shock and anger as she stared at Piers in stunned disbelief. From a long way away she heard Mrs Roberts' words of startled congratulations.

'You certainly had me fooled!' the housekeeper exclaimed, giving Piers a resounding kiss on the cheek. 'I had no idea at all.'

You weren't the only one, Fern thought furiously. Why didn't she say something, refute Piers' statement immediately? But she couldn't seem to think straight. And she knew that, if she did open her mouth, the words would pour out in an uncontrolled, incoherent, angry torrent.

She forced herself to smile as she in turn was embraced by Mrs Roberts.

'I'm so pleased,' she kept repeating, and did indeed look genuinely delighted, if still rather bemused. 'Now have you set a date yet? We could hold the reception here,' she continued contentedly. 'I can do the cooking and I'll ask Joan and Mary from the village to——'

'We'll sort out all the arrangements later,' Piers broke in smoothly. 'But right now I'm going to take Fern home . . .'

Mrs Roberts nodded understandingly. 'I expect you've all sorts of things to discuss.'

That was one way of putting it, Fern thought savagely.

'Come along then, darling.' Piers' eyes gleamed as he placed an arm tenderly around her shoulders and helped her to her feet.

'I can manage, thank you,' she said icily, shrugging off his hand immediately.

He smiled down indulgently at her. 'Pre-wedding nerves,' he murmured confidingly to Mrs Roberts, who smiled back sagely.

'I thought a fairly quiet wedding, if that suits you,' Piers said casually as he turned the ignition key and the car moved smoothly down the long, winding drive. 'Naturally I should like to invite the Robertses, and presumably you'll want Carrie to be present.' He glanced sideways at Fern. 'Shouldn't you be watching your blood-pressure, dear?'

'Will you stop this damn ridiculous charade right now?' Fern finally exploded, and then clutched frantically at the edge of her seat as without warning Piers swung on to the grass verge and slammed on the brakes. He turned towards her, his face grim.

'You think it's ridiculous that I should want my child to be born in wedlock?' he demanded curtly. 'You would prefer the baby to be illegitimate—like Carrie?'

'You bastard!' Fern said thickly.

'Rather an apt choice of word under the circumstances,' he grated, 'although as it so happens not one that strictly applies to me.' He paused. 'Fern, I can understand that you're angry at the moment.' His voice was more gentle now. 'I shouldn't have sprung this on you the way I did——'

'Oh, but I simply adore surprises!' Fern broke in caustically. 'I mean, it's not every day I'm informed out of the blue that I'm getting married. Except I'm not,' she added flatly. She smiled sweetly up into his face. 'So who's going to break the joyful news to Mrs Roberts that we've just terminated the shortest engagement on record?'

His mouth tightened. 'Why don't you stop thinking about yourself for five minutes, and think of the baby?'

She turned her head away as he started up the car again

and stared unseeingly out of the window. How shocked she'd been when Katherine had nonchalantly told her that she was pregnant. How ironic that she should herself now be in the same position, except—Fern's mouth twisted wryly—she at least knew who was the father of her child. Carrie had merely been the by-product of one of Katherine's numerous casual affairs. Fern bit her lip. She had never approved of her sister's lifestyle, but despite their differences she had still loved her very dearly. That was why it had been so much harder to bear when . . . Fern's eyes darkened as the tortured memories were unleashed.

Katherine and Steven. The two people she had once loved most in the world, and now they were both dead. She clenched her hands into white-knuckled fists. She had tried so hard to make her marriage work, to make Steven happy, but there must have been something missing in their relationship, something she had been unable to supply, something lacking in her. Only she hadn't been aware of it at the time. Naïvely she'd believed that Steven loved her, that she fulfilled him emotionally and physically. She'd trusted him implicitly . . . and he had betrayed her with her own sister. He had preferred Katherine, saddled with another man's child, to being married any longer to her.

Fern screwed her eyes shut. After the initial shock, anger and hurt had eased, she'd been left with the appalling knowledge that she'd been a total failure as a wife and a woman, that she hadn't been able to sustain a relationship for even three months.

Two weeks after Katherine and Steven had shattered her life, they had been killed in a car crash. Carrie on the back seat had escaped with minor injuries. At first Fern had recoiled from having anything to do with Katherine's baby, could hardly bear to look at her when she visited her in hospital. Then one day a nurse had placed the small, defenceless bundle in her arms and everything had changed. She'd realised that Carrie couldn't be held responsible for the past.

From then on, Carrie had become the reason to go on living. Fern opened her eyes, admitting the truth for the first time. She'd used Carrie as a buffer against the outside world, a perfect excuse for declining the invitations extended by well-meaning friends. She hadn't wanted to see anyone, had wanted to hide away in her own small world where no one could ever hurt her again. In those first anguished months, she'd faced the terrible truth that she would never trust another human being as long as she lived.

Fern gave a long-drawn-out sigh. And now Piers was asking her to trust herself and her baby into his care. A wave of pure terror engulfed her. She couldn't do it, couldn't go through with another marriage, even one where there would be no illustions to shatter.

'I can't force you to marry me.'

She jerked her head around as she heard Piers' cool, unemotional voice, frowning slightly as she realised that the car was parked in front of Thyme Cottage although she had no recollection of the journey home.

'I can hardly hold a shotgun at your back and insist you walk down the aisle.'

'The vicar might notice something amiss,' Fern agreed drily, relief surging through her. Thank heavens Piers had finally come to his senses and realised how impossible the whole idea was.

'But there's one thing I want to get quite clear. I intend my child to be brought up in my home, under my protection—with or without you.'

His child . . . it's *our* child. Without warning the words suddenly screamed in her head and in that moment she knew without doubt that she wanted this baby more than anything in the world. Then, as the full implication of what he'd said slowly registered in her muddled brain, and she glanced at the chilling angle of the tenacious, determined jaw, icy fingers reached out and clutched her heart.

'What?' she muttered uneasily.

'As soon as the baby is born I shall sue for custody,' he said crisply.

'You wouldn't . . . you couldn't!' Could he? Did he have any legal claim on the baby if they weren't married? Surely no court in the world . . .

'And I shall win,' he stated calmly. 'Money does have certain advantages,' he added drily.

'I'd deny you were the father,' Fern flared.

'Would you?' he asked quietly, and suddenly the fight went from her. No, she'd never be able to do that.

'Of course you would have visiting rights,' he continued and then shrugged. 'The choice is yours, Fern.'

'What choice?' she said bitterly, knowing she was defeated and hating him so much it was like a physical pain.

'I'll go ahead with the necessary arrangements, then,' he said evenly.

'As you like,' she answered drearily.

An expression of utter weariness crossed his face. 'I'm no happier about this situation than you, believe me.' His mouth curved wryly. 'It's hardly a marriage made in heaven, as Mrs Roberts might put it.' He paused. 'But I am determined to do everything within my power to ensure that my son or daughter is raised in a secure and happy environment.'

An environment as far removed as possible from the one in which he'd spent his own childhood, Fern thought silently. She'd been so preoccupied with her own problems that this was the first time she'd even considered how Piers must be feeling. He must be as reluctant as she was to enter into this cold-blooded union.

'And, for that reason, I want this marriage, at least on the surface, to be conventional.'

'You mean you'd prefer it if people didn't know that you'd virtually blackmailed me into it,' Fern said cuttingly. 'You'd like me to play the part of the misty-eyed, ecstatic bride?'

'I'd settle for civility.' He quirked a dark eyebrow at her.

She stared down at her folded hands. He was right, of course. They couldn't go on fighting—and play happy families! There wasn't just the baby, but Carrie to consider as well. Neither was exactly going to be happy placed in the middle of a battlefield.

'Truce?'

'I suppose so,' she muttered resignedly.

'Shall we shake hands on it, or would you prefer to seal it with a kiss?'

Her stomach lurched unexpectedly as her eyes flickered from the taunting blue eyes to the firm, straight mouth. 'Right now, I should prefer to go indoors and make myself a cup of tea,' she retorted coolly.

'I do hope marriage isn't going to impinge too much on your exciting lifestyle,' he drawled mockingly as she opened the car door and slid out. 'Car keys?' he called out after her stiffly erect, retreating figure.

'Sorry?' She turned round uncomprehendingly.

'I'll drive your car over later. Bert Roberts can follow in mine and take me back to Avonbrook.'

'How thoughtful,' she muttered, tossing the car keys through the open window on to the driver's seat, and instantly regretted both the heavy sarcasm in her voice and the churlish action. It *had* been thoughtful of him to remember her car which she would need later to fetch Carrie. So why couldn't she have just thanked him and handed over the car keys graciously? Why did he always arouse this fierce, burning antagonism inside her, making her over-react to even the simplest things he said or did? Chewing her bottom lip, she watched him drive away, and then, shoulders drooping despondently, she walked back towards the cottage.

It was by no stretch of the imagination what Fern would have termed a quiet wedding.

A fixed, jaw-aching smile hid her inner rebellion as she stood dutifully by Piers' side, greeting the seemingly never-ending stream of people who poured through the open glass doors into the plush hotel reception-room.

She should have taken more interest in the arrangements, she admonished herself bitterly, instead of leaving everything to Piers. But she'd acted like the proverbial ostrich over the past two weeks. It had been as if by trying not to even think about the forthcoming marriage, it would never happen.

Piers, much to her surprise, had insisted that the ceremony should take place in the local parish church, and although she would have preferred a register office Fern had acquiesced after only a token resistance, chiefly because she didn't have the heart to disappoint Carrie, who seemed to have taken it for granted that she was to be a bridesmaid.

'Surely there's someone you want to invite?' Piers had queried her failure to proffer any names for the guest list. 'Friends? Relatives?'

'No,' she had answered stubbornly.

'Not even your parents?' There had been an odd expression in his eyes that she'd been unable to analyse.

'They're in Australia.' She'd shrugged. 'We've never been very close. I'll write to them afterwards.' She'd paused and sighed. 'I have a bachelor uncle in Devon. I'll ask him to give me away,' she'd reluctantly made the one concession. She had just wanted to get the whole farcical ceremony over as quickly as possible and with the minimum amount of fuss. And she'd automatically assumed that Piers would feel the same.

Then, when she'd arrived at the church earlier that morning, she'd been stunned to discover that it was packed, a sea of unfamiliar faces turning towards her as she moved dazedly down the aisle. She must have come to the wrong church, she thought with a bubble of hysteria, but there was no mistaking the tall figure waiting for her on the chancel steps.

Piers looked magnificent in the dark, superbly tailored suit, brilliant white shirt and sober tie, she acknowledged with a painful lump in her throat. Already she was bitterly regretting that last-minute perverse decision to wear the severe beige suit instead of the cream silk dress with pink trimmings that she'd bought especially for the occasion. She didn't feel like a bride, she didn't look like a bride, but hadn't that been her intention? She'd had this childish desire to make it quite apparent to Piers that she was here under duress and not through free choice. And the whole thing had backfired on her. She saw the cold glitter in Piers' eyes as she reached his side, sensed his anger and disapproval and, instead of victorious, she just felt drab and miserable.

'Who are all these people? Rent-a-crowd?' she demanded as they drove from the church to the hotel for the reception. She was conscious of how aggressive she sounded, knew too that the aggression was merely a blanket to camouflage the strain and deep, gnawing unhappiness.

'Friends. Mostly relatives. On my mother's side,' he answered curtly, then turned his head dismissively and looked out of the window.

Fern absorbed the startling information in baffled silence. She'd just assumed that David was Piers' only blood relative; it had never occurred to her that she was marrying into a large extended family. But what on earth had prompted Piers to invite these relatives, most of whom he couldn't have seen for years, to share in this mockery of a wedding? It defied all reason, was totally incomprehensible.

She flicked a tentative sideways glance to the silent man by her side, her heart dropping as she studied the grim profile. If only he'd smile at her, make some flippant comment to ease that awful tension between them. Was this an indication of how they were going to spend their married life, she wondered drearily, only speaking to each other when absolutely essential, acting out their role of a happily married couple in public, but reverting to cool, impersonal strangers in private?

Fern's lips formed the polite words of acknowledgment as she was introduced to yet another of Piers' cousins and her husband. The young couple kissed her on the cheek and murmured the usual platitudes, but she could see the astonishment in their eyes, knew that they were baffled by Piers' unlikely choice of bride. They would learn the answer to their unspoken question in due course, Fern thought bitterly.

She looked up at Piers out of the corner of her eye. He deserved an Oscar for his performance, she admitted grudgingly. No one would suspect the strain he was under. He looked relaxed and self-assured, his eyes gleaming with amused tolerance as he counteracted the good-natured ribald remarks made by some of his male relatives with his innate dry humour. He looked like the man she had first laid eyes on down by Ladies' Pool, Fern realised with a sharp pang, the man with the teasing blue eyes who had kissed an unknown girl for the sheer devilment of it and because he thought she had beautiful hair. She was disturbed to realise how vivid that memory still was, and even more disturbed that the memory should prove to be quite so extraordinarily painful.

At least this part of the ordeal would soon be over, Fern thought thankfully. There couldn't be many guests still to arrive. Her eyes wandered back to the open door and widened in sheer disbelief, the fixed smile torn from her lips as the final couple came sauntering towards her. It wasn't possible! Surely not even Piers could be so insensitive as to ask Sally Thornton to his wedding! Had she been present at the church? Fern wondered frantically. No, even in her dazed condition she couldn't have failed to miss the girl in the dazzling jade-green dress. Green! Fern felt the swirl of hysteria curling up inside of her. Wasn't that supposed to be an unlucky colour to wear at a wedding? Dimly, she registered the tall red-headed man by Sally's side as being Piers' best man, the family resemblance between him and Sally now obvious.

Her heart seemed to stop beating as she watched Sally smile up at Piers.

'Congratulations,' she murmured huskily, and then stretched up and brushed his mouth with her lips.

That's my husband you're kissing! For one awful second, Fern thought she had uttered the words out loud, appalled by the wave of possessiveness flooding through her. She wanted to look away but couldn't. She saw the expression in Piers' eyes as he gazed back down at Sally and felt as if someone had stuck a knife into her back, the pain was so acute. This girl would have been Piers' choice of bride. Dear God, she wondered desperately, how long would it be before Piers started hating her, started blaming her for trapping him into this marriage, conveniently forgetting that it was he who had insisted on it?

'I'm going to find Carrie,' she murmured chokingly. She started to walk away and then some instinct made her glance back over her shoulder. Sally was staring after her, and the expression on her face sent an icy chill running down Fern's spine. How would she have reacted, Fern wondered dully, if their roles had been reversed—if Sally had married the man *she* loved . . . if Sally had married *Piers*?

Her mind whirled in small, frantic circles. The tension had finally proved too much; she was cracking up. Dazedly she headed for the powder-room, relieved to find it deserted, and sat down weakly on a red velvet stool. Uneasily, she stared straight ahead into the mirror. She was burning inside; her head felt as if it was going to explode and yet her face looked so calm and composed. It was her dark-fringed eyes that betrayed her, the two grey pools of bewilderment and fear. The door swung open, and quickly Fern retrieved her lipstick from her small purse and then relaxed as she saw the flushed reflection of Mrs Roberts.

'Think I've had one sherry too many,' the older woman confessed sitting on the adjacent stool. She removed her hat and fanned her face with a hand, then sighed contentedly. 'Carrie looks so sweet in that pink dress.'

Oh, heavens, she was supposed to be looking for Carrie.

'Bert's keeping his eye on her right now,' Mrs Roberts continued as if sensing Fern's unspoken query. 'Now, mind you don't go fretting about her while you're away in Jersey. I'll take good care of her.'

'I know you will,' Fern said warmly. 'It's so kind of you to——'

'I'm looking forward to having a youngster about the place,' the older woman cut in happily, and beamed. 'After all, it's not every day you go on a honeymoon, is it?'

'No,' Fern agreed with false brightness, absently blotting her lips with a tissue before remembering that she hadn't yet applied any fresh lipstick.

The week in Jersey had been another of Piers' bombshells. She had considered that a honeymoon was going to farcical extremes, but had protested only half-heartedly when Piers had coolly informed her two days ago that it was a *fait accompli*, that he had already made all the arrangements, evidently not having thought it necessary to even consult her. How on earth could she have been so wet as to give in so feebly? Fern now wondered in disbelief. She'd acted like a lump of mindless jelly over the past two weeks, she slowly registered. It was as if she'd been shell-shocked; nothing had seemed real any more. And now she had come to her senses it was too late to change anything. Harsh reality was the gold band on her third finger . . . Piers . . . her new home at Avonbrook . . . and the honeymoon.

She crushed the tissue in her hand as a wave of sheer panic shuddered through her. She was terrified, she realised desperately. Not of the uncertain, bleak future that lay ahead, not of Piers—but of herself, and those piercing feelings, as agonising as a physical pain, that kept tearing through her.

Other than asking courteously if she wanted a soft drink, Piers didn't speak to her at all on the short flight from Bournemouth to Jersey.

It was late evening when they arrived on the island, the sun shimmering on the tranquil sea as Piers drove the hire car along the coast road out of St Helier. Fern shot him a wary glance. What was he thinking about? she wondered. Was he resenting the fact that it was she who was by his side and not Sally? She bit her lip, turning her head away despondently. How was she going to get through the next seven days with this morose stranger who seemed barely aware that she even existed?

Piers branched left up a narrow, ascending road, a panoramic view unfolding below them.

'Gorey harbour,' Piers murmured. 'And that's Mount Orgueil Castle. It'll be floodlit once it's dark.'

So he hadn't taken a vow of silence, Fern thought wryly. But his voice had been as impersonal as if he were a travel courier. It was evident, too, that this wasn't his first visit to Jersey. He had driven with his habitual assurance from the airport without once pausing to consult the map provided by the hire-car company.

She frowned, puzzled, as he turned sharp right and drew up in front of two imposing wrought-iron gates. He wound down the car window, murmured something into the intercom on the red brick wall, and the gates swung open smoothly in front of them.

The car moved slowly forwards up a shrub-lined drive and Fern drew in her breath sharply as she saw the large, whitewashed house ahead of them, set amid green, rolling lawns, interspaced with flower-beds ablaze with vivid colours.

'Belongs to a friend of mine,' Piers said laconically.

'We're staying with your friend?' Fern's heart plummeted. She had taken it for granted that they would be spending the week in a hotel. She couldn't face meeting any more strangers today.

'Not exactly. Andrew lets the house during the summer.'

To extremely affluent holidaymakers, Fern decided.

'I thought you'd find it easier to relax here than in a formal hotel,' Piers added quietly, drawing up in front of the house.

Perhaps he was right, Fern thought silently. At least there would be no need to put on an act in this large, secluded house. They could fight as much as they liked and nobody would be any the wiser.

As Piers helped her out of the car, the front door opened and an olive-skinned woman with glossy black hair came down the steps towards them.

'Señor Warrender!' she exclaimed in recognition.

'Hello, Maria.' Piers greeted her with a warm smile. 'This is Señora Warrender.'

Beaming, the woman produced a small posy of flowers

from behind her back and pressed them into Fern's hand.

'Thank you.' Fern smiled back, touched by the gesture and then frowned, shaking her head uncomprehendingly as Maria burst into a torrent of rapid Spanish. To her astonishment, Piers intervened, talking fluently to the dark-haired woman in her native tongue.

'She wishes us a long and happy life together, blessed with many children,' he translated, quirking an ironic eyebrow at Fern. 'I thanked her for her good wishes,' he added drily.

'Oh, I see.' Soft colour washed over Fern's face as she buried her nose in the sweet-scented flowers.

'Maria and her husband have only been in Jersey six months,' Piers explained as, evidently familiar with the layout of the house, he ushered her into a spacious living-room, dominated by french windows leading out on to a terrace. Beyond lay an oval-shaped swimming-pool. 'José could speak English before they came, but Maria is only just beginning to learn.'

Fern wandered over to the french windows and gazed out. 'Does she get very homesick?' she murmured. She wanted to prolong this safe, neutral conversation for as long as possible, didn't want Piers to close up again.

'Apparently not,' he answered. 'Her life seems to revolve around José. I think she'd be happy wherever he was.'

'A dangerous trap to fall into,' Fern muttered almost to herself, unconscious of just how bitter she sounded. Never again was a man going to form the nucleus of her world. She glanced over her shoulder at Piers, and was momentarily disconcerted by the strange, fleeting expression that crossed his face.

'Would you like some tea?'

'Yes, please.' Her voice was as coolly polite as his own had been. 'I'd like to shower and change first, though.'

'I'll ask Maria to show you the bedroom,' he said equably,

moving to the door. 'While I see to the luggage.'

As soon as Maria had departed, Fern sat on the edge of the bed and kicked off her shoes, wriggling her stockinged feet into the deep carpet. Absently, her eyes roved around the bedroom, absorbing the cream and gold décor and luxurious furnishings, conscious only of an overwhelming sense of relief that she was finally alone. Then, drawn like a magnet, she stood up and padded across to the glass door, finding it opened smoothly under her hand, and stepped out on to the balcony.

Shadows were creeping across the lawn, heralding the approach of nightfall. Far below, in the harbour, the dying sun's rays turned the sea blood-red. Night-scented stock pervaded the air with a haunting, fragrant perfume. Unbidden, a lump formed in Fern's throat. An enchanted evening made for lovers, she thought bleakly.

She sighed unconsciously and then stiffened as she sensed the male presence behind her. Hadn't it occurred to Piers to knock before intruding on her privacy?

'It should be another fine day tomorrow, judging by that sky,' he murmured softly, moving to her side.

'Yes,' she said shortly. She didn't want to remain out here with Piers in this dangerous, magical world that was creating havoc with her senses. Her eyes dropped to the lean, strong hands resting, palm downwards, on the balustrade. A pulse started to beat erratically at the base of her neck. Those hands had caressed her body, drugged her mind against reason, invoked some kind of madness within her.

'That must be Maria. I asked her to bring the tea up.'

Fern nodded, hardly registering his words, keeping her face averted as he moved past her and went to answer the summons at the bedroom door. She took a deep, controlling breath, schooled her features into an expression of utter indifference and turned back into the room, faltering as her eyes moved from the tea-tray, complete with two cups, to the tall figure bending over an open suitcase, extracting an armful of male clothing.

'Why don't you pour out the tea?' Piers suggested, casually walking over to the large fitted wardrobe.

Fern didn't move. She was amazed to discover how calm she felt.

'Do I gather from all this activity that you're under the misapprehension that I'm going to share this room with you? Or doesn't your own bedroom possess a wardrobe?'

Piers arranged a blue shirt on a hanger. 'Oh, didn't I tell you?' he drawled, keeping his back to her. 'It's an old Jersey tradition that two people share the same room on their wedding night.'

'What a quaint custom,' Fern murmured sweetly.

'In fact I believe that some couples are even reckless enough to share the same bed.'

He might find that humorous, Fern thought witheringly, but she most certainly did not, and, the sooner she extricated herself from this potentially dangerous situation, the better. Swiftly, she collected her handbag from the dressing-table and picked up the small canvas holdall containing her hand-luggage.

'Where are you going?' Piers had moved silently across the carpet and now stood barring her way to the door.

'To find another room, as this one appears to be occupied,' she said evenly.

'I'd rather you didn't.'

Her mouth went dry. 'Y-you're not seriously suggesting that I sleep with you?' Her voice wasn't as steady as she would have liked.

'Yes,' he said bluntly, a muscle flickering in his jaw.

Her grip on the canvas bag tightened. 'What's the matter? Is the thought of even one night's celibacy too much for you to take?' She regretted the sneering jibe instantly, saw his eyes darken and braced herself for the explosion, momentarily thrown off balance when she realised that the expression in his eyes wasn't one of anger, but of a more intangible emotion.

'Sleep was the operative word,' he said quietly. 'I'm asking you to share my bed, that's all.'

An unwanted disturbing image of herself lying beside Piers in that large bed swirled into her mind.

'Don't you trust me?' This time there was no mistaking the flicker of anger.

'Is there any reason why I should?' she demanded bitterly, and stiffened as she felt the strong, warm fingers curling around her hands.

'Fern, this is no way to begin,' he murmured gently.

'I should have thought it was the only way to begin—as we intend to continue.' She snatched her hand from his grasp. 'You virtually forced me into this marriage, which as far as I'm concerned is in name only.'

His face tightened. 'I don't intend to spend the rest of my life living like a monk.'

'Another spot of blackmail?' Fern said sarcastically. 'Either I assuage your desires like the dutiful wife or you'll find someone more accommodating?' She drew her breath in sharply, appalled to discover how close she was to tears. 'Well, do as you damn well like!'

'If you insist.'

Her reactions were too slow, she didn't move in time to escape the hand that clamped around the back of her neck, forcing her towards him. Her ineffectual protest was stifled by the hard mouth that scorched her lips in a fierce, bruising kiss that was devoid of any tenderness.

'The gentle art of persuasion?' she choked as he raised his head, perversely grateful for that tearing anger that numbed all other emotions.

He didn't answer but turned away abruptly, picked up her suitcase, and strode out of the door and along the landing. Fern, lips pressed together, followed more slowly.

He flung open a door to the left. 'I think you'll find this room ideally suited to your needs,' he said sardonically.

Fern moved past him, her eyes flickering from the narrow bed pushed against the far wall to the single armchair and limited wardrobe space. Although as luxurious as the larger one, this room was clearly intended for sole occupancy.

'Thank you,' she said crisply, depositing her handbag on the chair.

'I'll ask Maria to prepare the room.'

'No,' she intervened swiftly. Witnessing the inevitable surprise on the Spanish woman's face as she was requested to make up the prim single bed was something Fern didn't feel able to deal with at present. 'I'll do it.' She'd spotted a linen cupboard halfway along the wide landing.

He shrugged, half turned away and then paused, his face a blank mask. 'I thought we could walk down into Gorey later if that suits you. There are some excellent restaurants near the harbour.'

'I'm very tired,' Fern murmured evasively. The last thing she felt like doing was sitting opposite a grim-faced, silent Piers in an intimate, candlelit restaurant. 'I think I'll just have an early night.'

'As you wish,' he returned coolly, making no attempt to dissuade her. 'Would you like a tray brought up to your room?'

'I'm not hungry,' Fern said shortly.

'Are you feeling sick again?'

'No.' At least, not in the way he meant. 'Now, if you don't mind, I really am tired,' she added pointedly as he remained blocking the doorway.

'Goodnight,' he said curtly, and closed the door behind

him.

Fern crossed the carpet, picked up her handbag from the chair and sat down. Well, she had what she wanted, she thought drearily; a room to herself. Solitude. Privacy. So instead of the expected relief, why did she feel so empty? Why did she long to throw herself down on that horrid little bed and burst into tears?

Fern stretched out a hand, retrieved her wristwatch from the bedside table and then sat bolt upright as she registered the time. She had slept for over ten hours. Despite her conviction that she would lie awake all night, she must have fallen into a deep, dreamless slumber the moment her head touched the pillow.

She threw back the covers, slipped out of bed, and padded barefoot over to the window. The room was instantly flooded with golden light as she drew back the curtains. She leant her elbows on the windowsill and stared out over the immaculate front garden, rather regretting her loss of a sea view. And the balcony, she reminded herself wryly, and then drew her eyebrows together as she noticed that the maroon hire car that had been parked in the drive last night was missing. Piers must have moved it around to the garage, she decided, ignoring that tiny flicker of unease.

She showered swiftly, registering with relief that she wasn't experiencing any of the nausea that had plagued her over the past few weeks. In fact, her appetite seemed to have returned with a vengeance. She pulled a pink cotton top over her head and zipped up her denim skirt. The latter had always been slightly on the large size, but now seemed to fit her perfectly. Her body was changing already, she mused, looking downwards, and was quite unprepared for the rush of emotion that swept over her. She was carrying Piers' child . . . his son. It was totally irrational, but she knew it was going to be a boy—a boy with dark, wavy hair and brilliant cobalt-blue eyes.

Weakly, Fern sat down on the edge of the bed. She was going crazy . . . it must be something to do with her changing hormones. And she had better get a grip on those strange and disturbing feelings before she faced Piers.

A woman clad in overalls, busily dusting the hall table, greeted Fern cheerfully as she reached the bottom of the stairs.

'Dining-room's over there,' she murmured helpfully, seeing the younger girl's slight hesitancy.

'Thank you,' Fern smiled back. She paused for a moment, took a deep breath to brace herself and opened the door. Her apprehension had been unnecessary. The dining-room was deserted, the long, polished table set for one. Oddly deflated Fern crossed the carpet and sat down.

'Where is my husband?' she asked slowly and carefully as Maria appeared, beaming broadly. It was the first time she had referred to Piers as such, and it made her feel strangely self-conscious.

'Already gone,' Maria announced in heavily accented English.

'I see.' She kept the fixed little smile on her lips, conscious that Maria was looking at her expectantly, presumably waiting for instructions about breakfast.

'Just tea and toast, please.' She didn't seem to feel hungry any more.

Maria nodded and turned away. What must she think of this strange English couple? Fern wondered.

Mechanically, she helped herself to a glass of fresh orange juice from the jug on the table. Where had Piers gone? And, more to the point, when would he be back? Her eyes darkened moodily. Surely, as a matter of courtesy if nothing else, he could have told her about his plans for the day. Left her a note, or something, instead of letting her find out through Maria. She took a gulp of orange juice but it didn't seem to relieve that dryness in her throat. She felt so . . . so . . . Her fingers tightened around the glass and fought against the temptation to pick it up and hurl it against the wall. She was relieved she had resisted, as Maria reappeared with the toast and tea.

The selfish brute had even taken the car, she thought savagely. Well, she decided resolutely, she wasn't going to waste the whole day moping around the house, waiting for Piers to return. She'd start exploring the island on her own. There were such things as buses—and legs. After all, she was quite accustomed to being on her own. In fact, she convinced herself determinedly, she was *glad* Piers had gone out without her, and she didn't have to endure his company all day. She'd enjoy herself far more without him.

She glanced up absently as the door opened and then her eyes widened as the object of her thoughts sauntered casually into the room, whistling under his breath.

'Piers!'

He raised a dark, quizzical eyebrow and sat down in a chair opposite her. 'I'm touched by that little gasp of delight.'

'Surprise,' Fern contradicted him sweetly. 'Maria gave me the impression that you'd gone out.' She shrugged, just to show him how unconcerned she had been by the discovery. What Maria must have meant, she now realised, was that Piers had 'already gone' from the dining-room, having finished his breakfast.

'Oh, I see,' he drawled, helping himself to a piece of toast. 'You thought I'd packed up my bucket and spade and gone off to make sand-castles without you.'

Despite herself, Fern couldn't help grinning at the ludicrous picture Piers' words had conjured up in her mind.

'You may scoff,' he informed her solemnly. 'But my creative genius with sand is world-renowned.'

'I'm sure it is,' Fern said drily. Would she ever get used to his mood changes? It seemed impossible that the cold, remote stranger of yesterday had been transformed overnight into this man with the teasing blue eyes.

'Is there anything special you'd like to do today?' he was now asking her pleasantly.

'I hadn't really thought,' she murmured vaguely. And with sudden disquiet she admitted that she didn't much care what she did—as long as she was with Piers. Quickly she lowered her eyes and concentrated on buttering another piece of toast. That disturbing admission made a complete mockery of her earlier assertions.

'How about a trip to Herm, as it's such a glorious day?'

Fern wrinkled her nose, trying to remember what she had read about the small island in the flight magazine on the aircraft.

'I thought Herm was nearer to Guernsey?'

'It's about a twenty-minute boat-trip from St Peter Port,' Piers agreed. 'But there's a regular air service between Jersey and Guernsey.' He glanced at his watch. 'We'd better make a move if we're going, though.'

Fern swallowed the remains of her toast and jumped to her feet.

'Won't be long,' she promised, conscious of a warm flutter of happiness. If Piers' moods were erratic, hers were equally changeable, she mused, dashing up the stairs to her room. She frowned. In fact, she admitted uneasily, it would appear that her moods were dependent on Piers'.

Fern stooped down and picked up a handful of sand, letting it trickle through her fingers. 'It really is made up of hundreds and hundreds of tiny shells!' she exclaimed in delight.

'Perhaps that's why this is called Shell Beach,' Piers teased gently, dropping the canvas bag containing their respective towels on to the sand by his feet.

Fern grinned, surveying the sparkling white sand that sloped down to the clear blue water. It wouldn't be that difficult, she decided, to imagine that she was on some deserted Caribbean island.

'How about that swim?' Piers started to unbutton his shirt. 'We should have worked off lunch by now.'

Lunch had been a seafood salad, eaten outside the only inn on Herm. Afterwards they had explored the tiny village, and then taken a leisurely stroll around the island, following the cliff path that was wide enough to enable tractors—Herm's only motorised vehicles—to pass. Fern had been a little wary of Piers at first, wondering how long his good humour would last, dreading the moment when, without warning, he would suddenly revert to being that cold aloof stranger. But it hadn't happened. Piers had been a friendly, entertaining companion. There had been no reference to last night, no recriminations, no more advances, and slowly Fern had begun to relax, responding to his gentle teasing with increasing confidence.

A little self-consciously, Fern slipped off her skirt and top to reveal the pale blue swimsuit she was wearing underneath. As Piers gave her little more than a cursory glance, she was disconcerted to discover that mingled with her relief with a touch of pique.

'Ready?' he asked.

She nodded brightly, determined that he shouldn't suspect the way her stomach had lurched at the sight of him clad only in the brief, dark swimming-trunks. Keeping her eyes averted from the disturbing, bronzed body, she walked down to the water's edge.

After ten minutes in the icy water, Fern decided she'd had enough. Arms wrapped around her drawn-up knees, she sat on her towel and watched Piers cut through the waves with deceptive ease. She had always considered herself a highly proficient swimmer, but, Fern admitted honestly, she was out of Piers' league. With his broad shoulders, deep, powerful chest and long, lean legs, he had the perfect physique for a swimmer.

As Piers waded out of the sea and walked towards her, droplets of water glistening on the matted dark hair on his chest, the sheer force of his attraction made Fern's mouth go dry. Weakly, she fished into the canvas bag and retrieved her sun-oil, and concentrated on massaging it into her exposed skin.

Piers dropped to his haunches by her side. 'I'll do your back,' he murmured, 'or you'll burn.'

'Thanks.' With determined nonchalance, Fern handed him the plastic bottle, watching as he poured a measured amount into the palm of his hand. His touch on her bare skin was cool and impersonal, but she had to fight to control her breathing, to keep her muscles relaxed, conscious that Piers would feel any tautness in her shoulders and back.

'And now you can return the favour,' he grinned, handing her back the bottle. 'By fetching me an ice-cream.'

Fern nearly sighed with relief. For one awful, heart-stopping moment she'd thought he was going to ask her to oil his back!

'Chocolate if they have it,' he decided. 'And perhaps one scoop of strawberry as well?' he added hopefully.

'Pig,' she murmured kindly, rising to her feet. She strolled across to the unobtrusive wooden kiosk and returned with a plastic cup of tea for herself and a cone for Piers.

'Vanilla. Like it or lump it,' she told him with mock severity. 'It's all they had.'

She sat down and sipped her tea, wondering why she should find the sight of the strong, rugged man beside her, licking the rapidly melting ice-cream with obvious relish, so oddly endearing as well as funny. Perhaps it was because

Piers simply looked so human.

'You've got ice-cream all over your chin!' Fern laughed softly as he finished the cone.

He wiped a lean hand across his mouth and grinned across at her. 'Better?'

As she met the dazzling blue eyes, Fern's heart constricted. 'You'll pass,' she said gruffly, looking away quickly.

They took the evening ferry back to St Peter Port, had a quiet meal in an unpretentious but excellent restaurant situated up a narrow cobbled street, and then caught the small yellow islander aircraft back to Jersey.

'Coffee?' Piers enquired as he opened the door of the house and flicked on the hall light.

'No, thanks,' Fern murmured, stifling a yawn. 'I think I'll go straight up.'

'Goodnight,' Piers said softly, taking a step towards her. For one second Fern thought he was going to kiss her, but instead he stretched out a hand and touched her cheek. 'You've caught the sun today.'

'You mean my nose has gone a tasteful shade of red,' Fern grinned, conscious of a feeling of anticlimax. In a day or two, she thought ruefully, her nose would probably start to peel.

She was wrong. Her nose didn't peel. Over the following days, Fern developed a uniform warm golden tan. The ludicrous paper nose-cap that Piers had solemnly presented to her over breakfast on their second morning had proved to be unnecessary.

Fern grinned at the memory, her eyes resting on the small, folded scrap of paper on her dressing-table, wondering why she had even bothered to keep the ridiculous thing. Absently she sat down on the stool in front of the mirror and started to brush her hair. It seemed impossible that this was her last night on Jersey, that the week she had so dreaded could have passed by so quickly and easily, each long, lazy day drifting into the next, time seeming to lose all meaning.

With Piers by her side, she had explored the rocky coves at the north of the island, scrambled down to the Wolf Caves, watched the sea swirl in a frenzy of white angry spray at the Devil's Hole. Together they had sauntered along the long stretch of beach at St Ouen watching the surfers, hunted unsuccessfully for crabs in the rock pools at Rozel Bay, swum in the small, secluded cove at Bonne Nuit. Sometimes, they had meandered inland, past solid stone farmhouses and small fields dotted with tethered Jersey cows, the deer-like breed that had been native to the island for hundreds of years.

Sighing, Fern put down her brush and padded over to her bed, switched off the light, and lay on her back staring up into the darkness. Piers had treated her with unfailing courtesy over the past few days, even kindness, but rarely had their conversation strayed beyond light superficialities. Never once had he mentioned his past life, or, Fern acknowledged uneasily, referred to the future. Perhaps, like her, he had simply been taking each day as it came, not wanting to think too deeply of all the problems that lay ahead. On occasions she had caught him studying her with dark, speculative eyes, but she'd been no nearer guessing at his thoughts than before, no nearer to really knowing the enigmatic man who was now her husband than she'd been on the fateful day she'd first met him.

And tomorrow they were going home. No. She'd never be able to think of Avonbrook as her home. It was Piers' house, the house he'd planned to share with Sally. She bit her lip. She didn't know that for a fact, did she? So why torture herself with such pointless speculation? If only she could fall asleep . . .

She stretched out her hand and switched on the bedside lamp, picking up the paperback novel she was halfway through. Perhaps reading would induce drowsiness—or at least keep her over-active mind occupied. Five minutes later she slammed the book shut. She simply couldn't concentrate.

Sighing, she threw back the bedcovers and grabbed her robe from the back of the door. She'd go downstairs and make herself a hot drink. Quietly, she stepped out on to the landing, automaticaly glancing towards Piers' door. There was no revealing thread of light under the door. He must be sound asleep, she thought enviously.

Silently she moved down the stairs and frowned as she noticed the soft glow issuing from the living room. Piers must have omitted to turn off the light before going to bed, she decided, padding quietly along the hall to rectify the error. Then, as she glanced through the open door, she went rigid.

Piers was slumped in one of the armchairs, long legs stretched out in front of him, eyes closed, a glass of whisky clasped in his right hand. Fern remained motionless, her eyes widening with shock as she saw the deep lines of unhappiness and strain etched in his face.

She hadn't made a sound, but some sixth sense must have alerted him to her presence and his eyes flickered open.

'Fern,' he muttered thickly, as if he were having difficulty in remembering her name. He took a sip from the glass. 'My sweet, loving wife,' he added bitterly.

'Y-you're drunk,' Fern said unsteadily. There was no feeling of disgust, just sheer bewilderment at his uncharacteristic behaviour.

He gave a low, mocking laugh. 'Unfortunately, that blissful state of oblivion seems to be eluding me.'

She didn't wait to hear any more. Blindly, she turned away and fled back up to her room, her original mission dismissed totally from her mind. Piers was drinking to forget . . . to numb his mind to the fact that . . . that he was married to her!

She sat on the bed and buried her face in her hands. How was it possible to hurt so much and still go on breathing?

There had been times during the last week when she'd almost been happy, when she'd believed that Piers was actually enjoying her company. And all the time . . .

Fierce, scalding tears burnt her eyes, bitter nausea choked in her throat. The knowledge that she was the cause of his obvious intense unhappiness was almost more than she could bear.

'Because I love him,' she whispered hoarsely. There was no sudden, shattering flash of revelation, just a dreary acceptance of something she had known for days—no, weeks—but had refused to admit. Deliberately she had chosen to ignore all the warning signals, telling herself repeatedly that she loathed the caustic, mocking man who had intruded into her orderly life. She'd fought him at every possible opportunity—and all the time she had been fighting herself. Even after she had physically expressed her love for him, she'd still been too stubborn—or was it too terrified?—to admit the truth.

She pressed a knuckle to her mouth to muffle the moan of despair. Oh, God, what a mess it was. She was in love with a man who had married her solely to protect his unborn child. A man who didn't even much *like* her, who had never shown her anything more than a brief, transitory desire.

Fern lifted her head and stared bleakly ahead. How was she going to endure waking up day after day knowing that she was ruining Piers' life, knowing how much he must resent her presence in his home, waiting for the inevitable day when that resentment changed to hate?

CHAPTER SEVEN

AS SHE approached the kitchen, Fern heard the rumble of Piers' deep voice followed by a shriek of laughter from Carrie.

'And then what happened?' Carrie demanded eagerly, oblivious to her aunt's silent entry. She was kneeling on a chair, the bowl of cereal in front of her forgotten, her eyes glowing with anticipation as they rested on the lean figure opposite her.

'The giant hedgehog——' Piers broke off, glancing over the small brown head. 'Good morning, Fern.' His voice was equable but the relaxed, good-humoured expression had vanished from his face. Carrie, too, had stiffened, her eyes watchful as she turned her head to greet her aunt.

'Carrie, how many times do I have to tell you to sit up properly at the meal table?' Fern reproved her sharply, moving across the tiled floor. Did Piers have to tell Carrie those ridiculous stories over breakfast every morning? And was it necessary to have the radio blaring out like that? Swiftly she turned the knob off.

'I was waiting to hear the news,' Piers said quietly as she sat down beside Carrie.

Fern didn't answer, but poured herself a cup of tea, conscious of just how quiet it was now in the kitchen. She frowned. Had she imagined that quick, almost conspiratorial glance that had passed between Carrie and Piers?

'I won't be in for lunch today,' Piers broke the strained silence eventually. 'But I'll be back in time to take Carrie to the stables,' he added. The riding lessons had been a present from Piers on Carrie's seventh birthday, ten days ago.

'Are you going over to see the owls again?' Carrie asked innocently.

As Fern saw him give a quick affirmative nod, her muscles tensed. That was the sixth time he'd been over to the owl sanctuary since their return from Jersey. She found difficulty in swallowing her piece of toast. And why did Piers have to keep on pretending that it was the owls that interested him? Couldn't he at least be honest and admit he was going to see Sally?

'Can I come with you?' Carrie asked hopefully.

'You know we've arranged to go into Bournemouth this morning to get your new school shoes,' Fern said quickly before Piers could answer.

'Couldn't we go tomorrow?'

'No,' Fern said shortly. Even as she spoke, she knew how cold and insensitive she sounded, knew too that there was no earthly reason why the trip couldn't be postponed until the following day.

'I don't want to go stupid old shopping with you.' Carrie stuck out her lower lip rebelliously. 'I want to go and see the owls.'

'Perhaps you can come next time,' Piers said quietly, smiling gently across the table.

Fern threw him a furious glance. This was between herself and Carrie. She didn't need him to try and act as peacemaker. If he'd never mentioned the owl sanctuary none of this would have happened anyway.

'But I'll be back at school next week. It's not fair——'

'That's quite enough, Carrie,' Fern said curtly. 'Now hurry up and finish your breakfast, please.'

'Don't want it. I hate cereal.' Carrie slung her spoon down on the table.

'I think you'd better go up to your room until you can learn how to behave properly.' Fern tried to speak calmly, fighting her own growing temper. How had this become so out of hand? she wondered desperately.

Scraping her chair back noisily on the floor, Carrie scrambled to her feet, her chin trembling with the effort of keeping back the tears. With slow, dragging steps she walked over to the door and disappeared into the hall.

Fern felt sick. She couldn't ever recall punishing Carrie in this manner before. There had never been the need. The seven-year-old had always been an even-tempered, good-natured child, open to reason. She had never been prone to temper tantrums, or wilful, deliberate disobedience. Fern's eyes darkened. At least not until now. Since they had moved into Avonbrook, Carrie had undergone some fundamental character change. She'd become sulky and argumentative.

'She's become impossible,' Fern muttered. 'And it's all your fault,' she flared at the silent man opposite her.

For a second, Piers surveyed her with narrowed eyes, his mouth drawn in a hard, straight line, and then wordlessly he rose to his feet and strode out of the kitchen.

Fern stared at the closed door, her hands clenched into fists in her lap. The anger had gone. There was just an aching emptiness inside of her. That look of utter contempt on Piers' face . . . She began to shudder uncontrollably. He was beginning to hate her already.

Numbly, she rose to her feet and started to collect up the dirty crockery and place it in the dishwasher Piers had installed shortly before Mrs Roberts had departed on a fortnight's holiday to Tenerife. She picked up the blue milk jug and somehow it slipped from her stiff fingers and crashed to the floor. Fern stared down at the fragments of china and burst into tears.

It wasn't Carrie who was impossible to live with, it wasn't Carrie who had changed . . . it was *her*. Sobbing, she knelt down and began to pick up the pieces of milk jug. She was the one who had been behaving like a self-centred, ill-tempered child ever since she'd returned from Jersey just over three weeks ago, lashing out at everyone around her as if somehow that would ease the pain inside her. And all she'd succeeded in doing was hurting a bewildered Carrie, who'd already had to contend with a dramatic change in her life, and making Piers despise her.

Fern wiped a hand across her eyes, stood up and carried the remains of the milk jug over to the bin. When she'd opened the kitchen door that morning, Piers and Carrie had been sitting together, looking relaxed and happy. Within five minutes of her entry the whole atmosphere had changed, become charged with electric tension. With tearing shame, Fern recalled the expression of anxiety and apprehension on Carrie's face. Was it any wonder that her niece should have wanted to spend the morning with Piers rather than her? Was it surprising, too, that Piers should keep going to see Sally, that he should spend every evening working in his office to avoid being alone with a sulky, moody wife who bit off his head every time he spoke?

She seemed incapable of being in the same room as Piers without trying to provoke him into an argument, some deep perverseness in her craving a blazing row. Yet never once had he come near to losing his temper with her. He had ignored her caustic jibes, retreating behind a cold wall of complete indifference which had frustrated her even further.

Fern chewed her lower lip, her eyes dark with misery. Piers didn't even want her assistance in the office any more.

'You may as well know that I'm advertising for another secretary,' he'd informed her coolly a few days ago.

'But I thought we'd agreed that I'd start working again once Carrie was back at school.'

'You should be taking things easy.'

'I'm having a baby. That doesn't make me some kind of invalid,' Fern had protested vehemently. He wasn't concerned about her welfare; he simply didn't want to spend any more time in her company than was unavoidable. 'Lots of women go on working until—'

'I'm sorry but this isn't a matter for discussion,' he'd cut in curtly. 'I've made up my mind.'

'And what am I supposed to do all day?' she'd asked acidly, furious with his high handedness. 'Knit baby clothes?' She certainly wouldn't be needed to run the household. That was taken care of extremely efficiently by Mrs Roberts.

Piers had shrugged and walked out of the room.

Fern sighed and stared down at the gold band on her left hand. She loved Piers so much, she thought despairingly, and yet she seemed to be hell-bent on completely destroying what had never been more than a very tenuous relationship in the first place. The chasm between them was growing wider by the day; soon it would be too late even to attempt to breach it. What was the matter with her? she thought with sudden horror. Why was she being such a defeatist? She should be doing everything within her power to make this marriage work, should be fighting for the man she loved, not practically driving him into the arms of another woman.

'Aunt Fern?'

She spun round, her heart constricting as she saw the small, dejected figure standing in the doorway.

'I'm s-sorry.'

Fern moved swiftly across the floor, put her arms around Carrie and hugged her fiercely. 'I'm sorry, too,' she whispered. Never again, she vowed, would Carrie suffer because of her own unhappiness.

The young girl lifted her face. 'Could I have red shoes, do you s'pose?'

'I s'pose it could be arranged,' Fern grinned, ruffling the brown hair. 'Now, go and clean your teeth and change into your blue T-shirt. Oh, and fetch your jeans and hard hat,' she added with sudden recklessness. 'On the way back from Bournemouth, I'll drop you off at the sanctuary and you can go straight on to the riding stables with Piers.'

Carrie gave a whoop of delight and tore from the kitchen. Fern followed more sedately, uneasily aware that her rash decision hadn't been prompted just through a desire to please her niece. She raised her chin defiantly. Well, it really was high time she reminded Sally Thornton that Piers had a wife!

Several hours later, the shoes having been successfully purchased, and Carrie's hunger pangs assuaged with a hamburger, Fern drove along a narrow lane, closed in on either side by massive oak trees. The car dipped into a pot-hole in the road and stalled. Fern turned the ignition key, the engine made a small, whirring sound and went dead.

'What's the matter?' Carrie asked anxiously.

Fern held up her hands in resignation. 'I don't know,' she admitted. She opened the car door and slipped out. 'We'll have to walk the rest of the way to Sally's.' She locked up the car and studied it critically, ignoring the temptation to kick the tyres. There would be just about enough room for another vehicle to pass, she decided.

As they approached the small red-bricked house, encircled by fenced pasture, Fern gazed down ruefully at her dusty sandal-clad feet, conscious too of the trickle of perspiration trickling between her shoulder-blades. So much for arriving looking cool and confident! It couldn't have taken them much more than half an hour to walk from the car, but she was surprised at how weary she felt.

'Oh, look, Jessie has come to meet us.' With a cry of delight, Carrie dropped to her haunches and started to fuss a small, black mongrel, who obligingly rolled over on to its back and offered up its pink stomach to be rubbed.

Fern opened the wooden gate next to the cattle-grid and followed the well-worn path that led around the side of the house to an immaculate whitewashed stable block.

A Land Rover with an owl motif painted on its door stood outside a large barn and beside it, lost in a world of their own, were Sally and Piers. With a sinking heart, Fern admitted that Sally was even more attractive than she remembered, the sun glinting on her red-gold curls so that they formed a fiery halo around her head.

Piers was leaning against the Land Rover, his arms folded across his chest, listening to Sally with a smile of amusement hovering on his lips. As if to emphasise some point she was making, she placed a proprietorial hand on his arm, looking up into his eyes. She was dressed in blue shorts and a brief matching sun-top, her bare legs and arms smooth and sun-tanned.

Piers suddenly threw back his head and roared with laughter.

'OK, sweetheart, you win,' Fern heard him drawl clearly, and then, paralysed, she watched as Sally threw her arms around Piers' neck and kissed him resoundingly.

She wanted to avert her eyes, wanted to rush away, but her legs didn't seem to be functioning properly. And then it was too late to do anything, because Piers had seen her and was coming towards her.

'Fern, what an unexpected pleasure.' There was no hint of embarrassment in the deep, sardonic voice, although he must have known that she'd witnessed Sally's loving embrace.

'I've brought Carrie over to save you having to drive back to Avonbrook to fetch her.' Did that cool, composed voice really belong to her?

'How very thoughtful of you,' Piers murmured ironically. Fern gave him an icy glance. Did he think she'd deliberately come over to spy on him, to check up on him like some jealous wife? Well, hadn't she? something whispered in her head. And all her suspicions had been confirmed, she admitted with tearing pain.

'Well, *I* think it's lovely to see you,' Sally broke in. The warm, seemingly friendly smile was belied by the malicious glint in her green eyes, and the implication in her words. 'I keep telling Piers that he ought to bring you with him when he comes over instead of leaving you stuck at home.'

I'll just bet you do, Fern thought savagely, bestowing an equally sweet, insincere smile on the other girl.

'I've finally managed to persuade him to be the guest speaker next Saturday,' Sally continued blithely.

'Guest speaker?' Fern echoed before she could stop herself, and saw from the smug expression on the redhead's face that she had unwittingly walked into some trap. And just how much 'persuasion' had it taken? she wondered acidly.

'Hasn't Piers told you about the charity dinner to raise funds for the sanctuary?' Sally asked innocently. She flicked a glance at the man by her side. 'How many other little secrets are you keeping from your wife?' she asked teasingly.

'Fern and I don't have secrets from each other,' he returned easily. 'We share eveything, don't we, darling?' His words were spoken in a slow, lazy drawl but his eyes were like granite as they rested on Fern's face.

What did he expect her to do? she wondered bitterly. Deny his deceptively flippant words? Admit out loud to Sally that their marriage was a complete sham, that they rarely sat at the same supper table together, let alone shared the same bed at night? With a feeling of utter relief, Fern saw Carrie running towards them, the black mongrel at her heels.

The small girl hurled herself at Piers, greeting him with as much enthusiasm as if they had been parted for weeks not merely hours. An unexpected lump formed in Fern's throat as she thought of the countless times she had yearned to launch herself into Piers' arms with exactly the same joyous abandonment as her niece.

'I've some new red shoes,' Carrie announced excitedly. 'And then the car broke down and we had to walk for miles and miles——' she added dramatically.

'Don't exaggerate, Carrie,' Fern cut in quickly. 'The car stalled about a mile or so down the lane,' she explained, 'and I couldn't get it started again.'

'Why didn't you telephone me?' Piers asked quietly.

'It never occurred to me,' she said stiffly, puzzled by the odd expression on his face. She couldn't even remember if they'd passed a telephone box.

'A man stopped and asked if we wanted a lift,' Carrie chipped in obligingly.

'You didn't . . .'

'Of course not!' Conscious of Carrie's presence, Fern tried to keep the anger from her voice. Was Piers deliberately trying to make her look an irresponsible idiot in front of Sally? 'I'm not in the habit of getting into cars with strangers.' Just of marrying them.

Piers turned to Sally. 'May I borrow your tow-rope?'

'It's in the garage. There's a set of jump-leads, too, if you want them.'

Practical as well as beautiful, Fern thought churlishly, and gripped hold of Carrie's hand. 'C'mon, let's go and get in Piers' car.'

'See you Saturday night,' Sally called out after her. 'And next time you come over you simply must have a proper look around.'

'I'll look forward to it,' Fern returned, her voice as sugary as the other girl's had been. She knew there would be no next time. It had been an appalling mistake to come here today and she wasn't masochistic enough to want to repeat the experience. It wasn't Sally who needed reminding that Piers had a wife, she acknowledged drearily. It was Piers himself. Except she wasn't and never had been a wife to him in the accepted sense of the word, and that was a situation she didn't know how to even start attempting to rectify.

'Mrs Roberts is here.' A pyjama-clad Carrie hurtled through the door of Fern's bedroom and came to an abrupt standstill, her eyes widening with admiration. 'Oh, you look beautiful,' she breathed.

Smiling, Fern replaced the top on her lipstick, a soft, rich shade of ruby, the same colour as her new taffeta evening dress, and rose slowly from the dressing-table stool.

'Would you be an angel and tell Piers I'll be down in a minute?'

'OK.' Impulsively, Carrie threw her arms around her aunt's neck. 'You smell gorgeous too,' she murmured with pleasure. 'As nice as——' she wrinkled her nose reflectively '——as nice as Barney when he's eating his hay. Only different.'

'That is just about the loveliest compliment I've ever had,' Fern said solemnly, keeping a straight face until Carrie had departed on her errand. How would the manufacturers of the ridiculously expensive French perfume react to the news that their famous product had just been compared to the aroma of a small, brown pony munching dried grass?

Her grin faded, the nervousness that had been temporarily allayed by Carrie's appearance flooding back through her again. It would be the first evening she'd been out with Piers since they'd returned from Jersey, and she was feeling as jittery and tense as a teenager on her first date.

She'd visited the hairdresser that morning and had her hair expertly trimmed and blown dry in a new flick-back style. Experimentally, Fern moved her head from side to side and felt her hair sweep across her bare shoulders. The girl who had created the transformation had been enthusiastic about the result, and Fern had originally shared her pleasure. But now sudden doubts assailed her. Was the style too casual for tonight? Should she have arranged her hair in some more elaborate, sophisticated style? Uncertainly she studied her reflection in the full-length mirror on her wardrobe door. With that expression of deep foreboding in her eyes, she decided ruefully, anyone would think she was going to a funeral instead of to what was intended as an enjoyable social occasion. Any minute now, she admitted, she would lose her nerve completely and tell Piers she couldn't go to the dinner, plead a headache . . . Quickly, she retrieved her evening bag from the bed, composed her features so that they revealed nothing of her inner agitation, and walked to the door.

That superficial composure nearly collapsed completely when she saw Piers, dressed in dark evening clothes, waiting for her at the bottom of the stairs. He looked totally and arrogantly masculine and the sheer force of his attraction made her feel weak, set her pulses racing erratically. To steady herself, she gripped hold of the banisters and slowly made her way towards him, acutely conscious of his silent appraisal, the blue enigmatic eyes taking in every detail of her appearance, but betraying nothing of his thoughts.

'Are you ready?' he asked quietly as she reached his side.

'I'll just go and say goodnight to Mrs Roberts and Carrie,' she answered brightly—too brightly.

'I'll wait for you in the car.'

She nodded and turned towards the living-room door.

The short drive to the country club where the charity dinner was being held was conducted in silence, Piers' air of deep preoccupation discouraging any attempt at conversation by Fern.

They must be among the last to arrive, she realised as they

drew to a halt in the packed car park.

'Thank you,' she murmured politely as Piers opened the car door for her. His touch on her elbow as he guided her towards the club entrance was light and impersonal.

As they walked into the plush foyer, Sally detached herself from a group of people and came gliding towards them.

'You look stunning.' Piers smiled down casually at the redhead and Fern felt as if she had been kicked in the stomach. She gazed ahead rigidly, not wanting to see the look of admiration in Piers' eyes. Worst of all, Fern acknowledged, her muscles cramping, he was only speaking the truth. In the figure-hugging emerald-green dress with the deeply slashed neckline, Sally looked vibrant and provocative.

'You don't look so bad yourself,' Sally returned with easy familiarity. 'Hello, Fern,' she added as if she'd only just registered the other girl's presence. She touched Piers lightly on the arm. 'Now for heaven's sake go and mingle, will you?' She smiled up into his eyes. 'Most of these people are only here tonight because they're hoping to exchange a few words with the elusive P. Wolfe. Sorry, Piers, your cover is well and truly blown,' she said teasingly, 'but it's in a good cause.'

Fern was acutely conscious of the number of female heads that turned to assess the lean, dark-haired man by her side as they moved further into the reception area where cocktails were being served. She was aware, too, that it had nothing to do with his celebrity status. Piers would always command attention wherever he went. He wasn't the tallest man in the room, nor even the most handsome, yet he was easily the most compelling. His air of complete and utter self-assurance, that latent, potent virility seemed to challenge every woman to be the one he noticed. This is how it must feel to be married to a pop star or film idol, Fern thought, fighting the urge to giggle at the knowledge that she must be the object of some totally unwarranted envy.

'What would you like to drink?' Piers asked her quietly.

Treble brandy. 'Just a fruit juice,' she replied dutifully, and watched him walk away with the familiar, lazy loping stride. He seemed totally unconcerned by the number of sideways speculative glances he was attracting. Or perhaps, Fern thought wryly, he was so accustomed to that reaction that he no longer even noticed it.

'Hello, Fern.'

'David!' She spun round and smiled tentatively at the fair-headed man who had come up behind her. It had never occurred to her that David would be attending the dinner. Yet in retrospect, she realised, it wasn't so surprising. She'd already gauged that most of the prominent and influential families in the area were represented here tonight.

'How are you?' she asked cautiously. She hadn't seen him since the day she'd left the estate office. She'd written him a brief note shortly before the wedding, deeming it only fair to do so, but hadn't expected or received any acknowledgement.

'I'm fine,' he murmured, and she sensed that he was feeling equally awkward. 'And how's married bliss?'

'It's everything I imagined it would be,' she answered lightly.

'You're certainly looking very well.'

It was hardly the most lavish compliment in the world, Fern admitted wryly, but the look of male appreciation in his eyes went some way to restoring the confidence that had been badly dented by Piers' total indifference to her appearance that evening.

There was a long, strained pause and then they both spoke at once, and in the ensuing laughter the tension between them eased.

David started to talk about the estate, outlining various improvements he was planning to implement. Fern listened with interest, surprised to discover that now she was no longer involved with him she found David's slight pomposity amusing, almost endearing rather than irritating.

'I still haven't managed to find a replacement for you,' he concluded his monologue.

'But I thought . . .'

'Anne left after a month and went haring back to London. She decided that she wasn't cut out for country life.' He smiled. 'Too noisy in the morning and too quiet at night!'

Fern started to laugh, remembering her own initial dismay at being woken at daybreak each morning by the raucous dawn chorus outside her bedroom window.

'Good evening, David.'

The smile faded from her face as she heard the cool voice behind her.

'Your drink.' There was an icy glitter in Piers' eyes as he abruptly handed Fern a glass of fruit cocktail. 'We're just about to go into dinner,' he added shortly, and before she had time to register what was happening, let alone protest, she was being propelled across the room.

'That was damn rude,' she muttered in a ferocious aside, shrugging off his arm. 'I was talking to David.'

'About old times?' he mocked sardonically.

'As it happens, yes,' she lied sweetly, and saw his mouth tighten in a hard line. She could sense his anger and knew it had something to do with his strong antipathy towards his half-brother. Half of her resented the high-handed way in which he had practically dragged her away from David; the other half was childishly pleased that she had somehow, albeit unwittingly, managed to annoy him. Anything was better than indifference. At least now he had been reminded that she existed!

She was rather sorry to find that she wasn't seated near David at the long dining table, but joined in brightly with the light-hearted conversation around her, determined to distance herself from the man by her side. But, try as she might, she found it impossible not be be conscious of him. Even when she avoided looking at him and talking to him, every nerve in her body was painfully alive to his proximity.

Weakly, she flicked him a careful glance from under her thick lashes. He was chatting to a hitherto grim-faced woman sitting opposite him, who was visibly melting under his attention. It would appear, Fern thought wryly, that no female was immune to that masculine charm. It was something to do with the mesmerising blue eyes, the slow, lazy grin, the way Piers gave his total concentration to whomever he was talking to, making them feel for a few, all too brief moments that they were the only person in the world. At least, Fern decided with a touch of bitterness, that was how she imagined it must feel. Piers had never found it necessary to exert that charm on his mere wife.

After the last course was cleared away, and the replete dinner guests sat sipping coffee and liqueurs, Sally rose to her feet, graciously thanked everyone for their support of the owl sanctuary, and introduced Piers.

As he began to talk in his deep, drawling voice, Fern's eyes flickered around the table, absorbing the rapt faces. No one moved or fidgeted, the glasses of port and brandy forgotten.

Succinctly and fluently, Piers paid tribute to Sally's contribution towards conservation, detailing her work with the barn owls. There was an expression of deep respect on his face that sent a wave of despondency rushing through Fern, as she acknowledged that it wasn't just physical attraction that drew Piers to Sally.

Piers finished by relating a couple of hilarious anecdotes about his work as a wildlife photographer and sat down amid tumultuous applause. He turned his head and gave Fern a faintly quizzical smile.

'I think you were a big hit,' she murmured drily, longing

to reach out and touch his hand, to tell him about that almost unbearable rush of possessive pride that was surging through her. Possessive pride she had no earthly right to feel, she told herself sharply.

A small band started to play as the dinner guests filtered back into the reception area, and couples began to sway slowly in time to the beat.

'Shall we go?' Piers suddenly asked abruptly.

Fern shot him a puzzled glance. She had been mentally steeling herself for the sight of Piers and Sally entwined in each other's arms.

'Don't you want to dance?' she asked lightly.

'I've always found dancing a rather hazardous pastime,' he drawled. 'In fact, the last time I danced with a girl, I ended up marrying her.'

The unexpectedness of the teasing grin made Fern's heart skip a beat. It had been a very long time since Piers had looked at her like this, as if he were really seeing her.

'You know,' she murmured thoughtfully, 'I had a very similar experience myself.'

'Tell me about it on the way home,' he invited.

Fern tilted her head and smiled back up at him. For a moment her eyes were locked into his, and somewhere in the dark, blue, shadowy depths she glimpsed something that sent a tingle running down her spine.

'Good night, Mrs Roberts. And thanks again.' Fern watched as Piers settled the middle-aged woman into the car and then walked around to the driver's side. He wound down the window and stuck his head out.

'Shan't be long,' he called up to Fern. 'How about getting the coffee on?' he added with a grin.

Slowly and thoughtfully Fern went back into the house and through to the kitchen, cautioning herself against that warm rush of happiness that threatened to explode inside her. She switched on the kettle and moved across to the window, staring out into the garden, bathed in silver light. Just because Piers was being pleasant to her, had smiled at her, it didn't mean that anything had changed fundamentally between them. She mustn't start building up her hopes, analysing his every remark and expression, searching desperately for something that wasn't there.

It was puzzling that his attitude towards her had changed so dramatically during the course of the evening. But then, she mused ruefully, when had she ever been able to understand Piers Warrender?

She heard the sound of footsteps in the hall and quickly busied herself setting out two mugs, not wanting Piers to catch her in this dreamy state.

She glanced up at him as he filled the doorway.

'Leave the coffee,' he murmured quietly, moving towards her.

Fern's mouth went dry, her eyes riveted to his face, a pulse beginning to beat erratically at the base of her neck.

'Go and change into a pair of jeans and thick sweater.'

'What?' She couldn't believe she had heard him correctly. Was he quite mad? And for a moment she'd thought . . .

'I want to show you something. In the garden,' he drawled casually. 'Come on, hurry up,' he added impatiently as she remained rooted to the spot, staring at him with large, bewildered eyes.

If he was mad, it was obviously catching, Fern decided wryly as she sped upstairs to change, pausing instinctively on her way back downstairs to check on the sleeping Carrie.

'It's like daylight,' Fern murmured as she walked across the moonlit lawn by Piers' side. She flicked him a sideways glance. 'What is this all about?' she demanded.

'You'll see,' he said infuriatingly. Casually he reached out and took hold of her hand, leading her into the dense wooded undergrowth at the bottom of the garden that Piers had adamantly insisted should remain in its natural state.

There was nothing casual about Fern's response to the feel of the warm, lean fingers grasping hers, and she hoped fervently that Piers hadn't noticed that tremor that shivered up her arm.

'Stand still and listen.' Piers' mouth was next to her left ear.

At first all she was conscious of was the surge of adrenalin pumping around her body in response to Piers' intoxicating nearness, and then quite distinctly she heard a strange snuffling sound.

'What's that?' she whispered and then gripped hold of Piers' arm without thinking as a grey shape emerged from the undergrowth, followed by two smaller ones.

'Badgers,' she breathed, her mouth curving with delight as she gazed transfixed at the stout, broad-bodied mammals with the unmistakable pointed muzzles.

The sow raised her snout, sniffed the air and, seemingly unconcerned by the alient scent, continued slowly on her route, followed by the two cubs. As the small convoy disappeared into the shadows, Fern let out a long sigh.

'How did you know they'd be there?' she wanted to know as she and Piers retraced their steps towards the house.

'They've been coming into the garden most nights,' Piers explained. 'Encouraged by a few peanuts,' he added with a grin. 'For which they appear to have a strong addiction.'

'So that's why they weren't afraid of us,' Fern murmured. 'They've become used to you watching them.' She'd been aware of Piers' nocturnal rambles in the garden, but had assumed that they had been prompted by a desire for exercise and fresh air after sitting at his desk all evening. 'Where's the set?'

'Over there.' Piers waved a hand in the direction of the encompassing forest. 'Not too far away, actually. There's a couple of foxes tenanting the upper passages at the moment. Plus about a dozen or so rabbits.'

'And they all live together,' Fern mused wonderingly. She flicked Piers a glance, her eyes narrowing with sudden suspicion. 'What made you buy Avonbrook?' she asked with deceptive casualness.

'I was deeply attracted by the size of the kitchen,' he answered gravely.

Fern felt laughter bubbling up inside of her. 'You only bought the house because you knew there was a badger set nearby,' she accused.

'Guilty as charged,' he grinned, and suddenly grasped hold of both her hands and swung her around in front of him. 'Have you enjoyed tonight?' he asked abruptly.

'The last part, anyway,' Fern answered truthfully. She could see his face clearly in the moonlight and quite without warning felt giddy, weak with love for him. She tried to avert her eyes, terrified that he would read the message in them, but she seemed to be hypnotised by the compelling blue gaze.

'You're trembling,' he muttered, and slowly drew her towards him.

'Am I?' she choked, her breasts rising and falling in time with her erratic breathing as his hands moved to her hips, moulding her into his hard body. He bent his dark head and his mouth took possession of hers, parting her lips to taste the warm moistness within.

Feverishly, Fern kissed him back, the fierce, hungry longing of weeks finally undammed. Her arms lifted and locked around his neck, her fingers curling tightly into the thick, dark hair.

Dazedly she looked up at him as he raised his head, her lips swollen with passion, her eyes cloudy with desire.

Without speaking, he picked her up in his arms and strode towards the house, shouldering the front door open and kicking it shut behind him with a foot.

Fern buried her face against his chest, hearing the loud thud of his heart as he carried her up the stairs and along the landing to the master bedroom. Gently he set her down on the carpet, imprinting heated kisses on her temple and closed eyes, his mouth tracing a scalding path down her throat.

She offered no resistance as he swiftly eased her jumper over her head, drawing in her breath sharply as his hands cupped her breasts, his long, lean fingers sliding under the lacy bra and moving teasingly across the roused peaks.

Slowly and deliberately, he removed the remainder of her clothes and carried her across to the bed. He stood back, his eyes travelling over her naked, silken body, pale in the moonlight pouring through the window.

'You're so beautiful,' he murmured thickly. He knelt by her side, his mouth trailing sensuously down the length of her body, his lips and tongue flaming her nerve-endings. A little moan of pleasure escaped her and her body began to move restlessly under his caresses.

'Piers,' she choked, reaching out urgently to him, her hands fumbling at the buttons of his shirt. She wanted to explore his body as intimately as he was hers, needed desperately to feel him against her.

His clothes joined hers in a pile on the floor and he stretched his long body beside her on the bed, his mouth locked on hers.

Fern's hands moved over his shoulders, revelling in the feel of the warm, muscled skin, and then slid down his back as she arched herself against his body.

'Please, oh please,' she heard herself whisper, aching for that final fulfilment.

With a muttered groan, he lowered himself over her, Fern

instinctively raising her slender hips to meet the hard demand of his thighs.

He was gentle at first, and then the rhythm of his possession intensified, urging Fern with him up an ascending spiral of exquisite pleasure to the final shuddering release.

Fern blinked open her eyes drowsily and stretched her arms above her head, conscious of a sense of utter well-being and a peace more complete than she'd ever experienced before.

'Good morning.' Piers was propped on one elbow, watching her.

She smiled back at him, wondering if there could be anything more wonderful in the world than waking up beside the man she loved. It didn't seem to matter any more that he didn't love her. All that mattered was being with him like this, here and now. She didn't want to think any further ahead than that.

'What's the time?' she asked languidly.

'Early. Carrie won't be awake for hours,' he drawled teasingly, stretching out an arm and drawing her into the warm contours of his body. For a while Fern was content just to lay nestled against him, breathing in the male scent of his skin, cocooned in the security of his arms, glad that he seemed as disinclined to talk as she did. Then, as Piers began to stir against her, she felt the rekindling of her own desire, desire that soon flared to fever pitch under the skilful, expert hands.

When Fern woke for the second time, she found Piers, fully dressed, standing over her with a cup of tea in his hand. He placed the tea on the bedside table and, framing her face with his palms, kissed her lingeringly on the mouth.

'It's eleven o'clock,' he murmured, reluctantly releasing her lips.

'Oh, heavens,' Fern yelped in consternation. 'Why didn't

you wake me when you got up? Where's Carrie?'

'Everything's under control,' he grinned. 'Carrie's had breakfast and is playing in the garden. I told her you were having a lie-in after your late night,' he teased. 'And,' he added, his eyes roaming down the length of her body, clearly defined under the single sheet, 'I should hurry up and get dressed if I were you, otherwise Carrie might be having lunch on her own.'

Fern drank her tea thirstily as Piers left the room, and then, humming under her breath, borrowed his bathrobe and returned to her own room to shower and dress. She caught a glimpse of her reflection in the mirror and laughed softly as she registered the glowing eyes and flushed cheeks. Last night Piers had told her that she was beautiful—and today, she actually believed him.

She heard the sound of the doorbell as she walked along the landing and peered over the banisters curiously. Piers was walking towards the front door. He hadn't mentioned that he was expecting a visitor, she mused, and then stiffened as she saw him usher a smiling Sally into the hall and along to his office.

At least they hadn't closed the door behind them, Fern consoled herself, moving slowly down the stairs. There was nothing to get agitated about.

'Piers Warrender, I do love you.'

Sally's voice floated up the stairs, the words clear and distinct. There was a deep male chuckle and then silence. Images of Sally and Piers locked in each other's arms, kissing, touching, burnt into Fern's tortured mind.

Weakly, she slumped against the banisters, and stared numbly ahead. Last night had meant nothing to Piers. He'd needed to assuage his sexual desire and she'd been a convenient and willing body. She cringed, sick with revulsion and disgust. And now Piers was blatantly betraying her in their own home.

She couldn't remain in this house a second longer. Blindly she fled down the remaining stairs and across the hall. She flung open the front door, missed her footing on the wide steps and fell headlong on to the gravel. From a long way away she could hear someone screaming. And then realised it was she.

CHAPTER EIGHT

'YOU'RE young and healthy. There's no reason why you shouldn't have another child.'

No medical reason, perhaps. Listlessly, Fern gazed at the white-coated figure standing at the foot of the bed. It was the same young doctor who had gently broken the news to her that she had lost the baby. Was that yesterday or today? She seemed to have lost all track of time lying here in bed, wasn't even sure if it was morning or afternoon. It must be something to do with those tablets she'd been given to make her sleep.

A nurse started to plump up her pillows. 'Would you like to sit up? Your husband is here to see you.'

'I don't want to see him,' Fern said calmly.

'Now, you mustn't start upsetting yourself like this.'

'I'm not upsetting myself like anything,' she answered patiently. 'I simply don't wish to see my husband at the moment.' In fact, she had a feeling that once the grey fog cleared from her mind she wouldn't want to see Piers ever again. Only, right now, she didn't seem to be able to think straight, didn't seem to be able to feel anything except a curious numb emptiness.

'Mrs Warrender,' the nurse gazed at her earnestly, 'it was an appallingly tragic accident, but you mustn't feel guilty. You weren't to blame.'

Fern smiled. Did the nurse really think that she was blaming herself for the fall that had led to the miscarriage, and that was why she couldn't face Piers? How ridiculous. Because, she decided thoughtfully, it was actually Piers who was to blame. It was as much his fault as if he had placed his hand in the small of her back and pushed her down those steps. He was responsible for the loss of her baby . . .

'No!' Her fingers clutched the edge of the sheet, reality tearing through her like a knife. Turning her head into her pillow, she started to sob, her body racked with pain and anguish.

'Fern?'

She shrank from the hand that touched her lightly on the shoulder.

'Go away,' she muttered hoarsely, keeping her face averted. 'I told them . . .'

'That you didn't want to see me? Yes, I know.'

Slowly, she turned her head and gazed up at Piers. How ill and drawn he looked, she observed with cold detachment. And his voice had sounded so stilted and strained. He hadn't even said he was sorry about the baby yet, she thought with a rush of bitterness. He was just standing there, staring at her, his face a shuttered mask. But then he had never wanted this baby. Had never wanted her.

'How's Carrie?' she asked dully.

'She was shocked and upset at first, but Mrs Roberts is taking care of her.' He sat down in the hard-backed chair by the bed, looking stiff and uncomfortable, his hands splayed across his knees.

'The doctor said that unless there are any unforeseen complications you should be able to come home in a few days. You'll have to take things easy, though, and have plenty of rest.'

'I don't want to go back to Avonbrook.' Fern's eyes dilated with panic. 'I c-can't . . .'

'It's all right,' Piers murmured soothingly. He stretched out a hand and with uncharacteristic hesitation drew it back before he'd touched her. 'We can go away for a while if that's what you want.'

'No!' The last thing in the world she wanted was to go somewhere where she'd have to be alone with Piers. She stared up at the ceiling, and her mind suddenly cleared, her thoughts becoming lucid. 'I want go back to the cottage,' she stated decisively.

'What?'

She turned her head towards him. 'I'll go back to work for David. He's looking for another secretary. I'll be able to pay you rent. I don't expect or want any alimony from you.' The words tumbled out in short, staccato bursts.

His eyes narrowed, his mouth tightening. 'What are you talking about?'

'Divorce.' It was even more difficult to say than she'd imagined it was going to be. 'After all, we only got married because of . . .' she took a controlling breath '. . . so now there's no reason to carry on with the farce. The sooner we get everything sorted out, the better for both of us.' Her voice was calmer now, more controlled. 'Then we can both get on with our lives.'

'You're upset. You don't know what you're saying. We'll talk about this when you're feeling better.'

'I'm not ill,' Fern said icily. 'And I'm perfectly rational.' She shrugged. 'I know about you and Sally.' Her voice was devoid of all emotion.

'Know what exactly?' Piers asked ominously.

'Surely you don't want me to spell it out?' Fern muttered witheringly. 'Do you think I'm blind? I've seen the way she looks at you——'

'Sally is a flirt,' he cut in calmly. 'She looks at every man like that. Surely you've the sense to realise what she's like?'

'And does she kiss every man she meets and tell them that she loves them?' Fern enquired politely. She wanted to laugh at the expression on Piers' face. 'I heard her in your office,' she explained matter-of-factly.

Comprehension dawned in the blue eyes. 'Sally happened to "love" me at that precise moment because I'd agreed to write an article about the sanctuary for one of the Sunday supplements.'

'You don't expect me to believe that?' Fern scorned.

'You are at liberty to believe whatever you like,' he murmured unconcernedly. She heard the sudden, ragged intake of breath. 'My God, was that why——? Fern, you crazy little idiot . . .'

She recoiled as he scooped her into his arms, her hands pushing against the hard wall of his chest.

'Don't touch me.' Her voice shook with revulsion, the feel of his hands on her body making her feel sick. 'Not ever again.'

His arms fell to his sides. 'Don't shut me out, Fern. I want——'

'The only thing I want from you is my freedom,' she broke in vehemently, her eyes dark with loathing, hating him with all the passion she'd once loved him.

Piers rose to his feet in a jerky movement and looked down at her in silence, a muscle flickering in his jaw.

'This is hardly the time or the place I would have chosen to discuss the matter.' he said finally, his voice controlled and expressionless, 'but I agree with you. It is pointless prolonging this travesty of a marriage any further.'

He shrugged. 'You can have Thyme Cottage if that's what you really want. I'll change the deeds to your name as soon as possible.' He cut through her protests forcefully. 'If you can't bring yourself to accept it from me for yourself,' he said, a touch of bitterness creeping into his voice, 'do it for Carrie. She needs a permanent home.'

'Thank you.' It nearly choked her having to be grateful to

him, but for Carrie's sake she had to swallow her pride and keep her temper in check.

'There's just one condition,' he continued quietly. 'I'd like you to stay at Avonbrook until you're stronger. You'll need looking after and so will Carrie,'

It made sense, she admitted, although it would be unbearable returning to the house that had never been her home. 'Yes,' she agreed drearily. 'And now, if you don't mind, I'd like to go back to sleep.' She made a great pretence of snuggling down into the bed.

'I'll see you tomorrow.' There was a note of utter weariness in his voice

'There's really no need,' she said frigidly.

'I thought I'd bring Carrie with me, if you're feeling up to it. I think she'll be a lot happier once she's seen you.'

'Yes, of course.' Fern nodded quickly. 'Goodbye, Piers.' She closed her eyes, wishing it were as easy to shut him out from her thoughts.

It was a very subdued Carrie who appeared by Piers' side the following evening. She clung to Fern's hand, staring at her with wide, anxious eyes.

'I'm all right, darling,' Fern told her with a reassuring smile. 'And I shall probably be coming home the day after tomorrow.' She avoided Piers' eyes, and sighed inwardly. It wasn't going to be easy telling Carrie that she was to be uprooted once again.

'But why do we have to go back to the cottage?' the seven-year-old asked predictably when Fern broke the news to her some two weeks later. 'I like it here.' Carrie gazed around her pink and white bedroom, the walls of which were adorned with equine pictures, and her eyes filled with tears. 'What about all my horses?'

'You can bring them with you,' Fern murmured

soothingly, holding her close, letting her cry. She must start packing up her and Carrie's possessions. It wouldn't take long. She would take nothing that she hadn't brought with her to Avonbrook. The clothes she'd purchased as Piers' wife she would leave behind, or donate to a charity shop. She didn't want to keep anything that would remind her of Piers.

'Now go and wash your hands and face,' she said gently as Carrie's sobs subsided. 'Mrs Roberts has made one of her special chocolate cakes for tea.'

She had informed Mrs Roberts yesterday about her impending departure and had been surprised at how visibly shocked and upset the older woman had been. Fern had judged that Mrs Roberts of all people would be aware of the situation that now existed between herself and Piers.

Carrie's expression brightened considerably and she scampered off to the bathroom. Fern remained sitting on the small bed, smiling wryly. Apparently there was nothing much wrong with a world in which there was still chocolate cake for tea! She didn't delude herself, however, that Carrie had taken the news that easily. There would be more questions, more tears. But Carrie would soon adjust to living back at Thyme Cottage. She was young and resilient. Avonbrook and Piers would fade from her memory.

Fern stood up and walked over to the open window. Summer was drawing to an end, the haunting, melancholy scent of autumn already pervading the air. Would she ever be able to forget Piers? Would the day eventually dawn when she was completely free of him?

The weeks of her convalescence, of being waited on hand and foot by a motherly, concerned Mrs Roberts had done much to restore her physical health, but the enforced inertia had allowed her far too much time to brood. All she now longed to do was return to Thyme Cottage and start working for David again. She had telephoned him three days ago, and after expressing his initial surprise at her request he had been more than willing to reinstate her as his secretary. Maybe, Fern prayed desperately, once she'd resumed her old lifestyle, she would somehow manage to turn the clock back and shut out the past months as if they had never happened.

Slowly, Fern turned away from the window and walked out of Carrie's bedroom and down the stairs. She could hear raised voices coming from the office, and as she reached the hall the office door burst open and a young woman stormed out. She pushed past Fern, muttering under her breath, and marched out of the house.

Fern raised her eyebrows at Piers who was standing in the hall, arms folded imperiously across his chest, his face as black as thunder.

'Another personality clash?' she enquired drily. It was the fourth secretary who had walked out on Piers in the past fortnight. In fact, this last one's duration of three days had been a record.

'Why does that bloody agency persist in sending me neurotic females who can't spell or type?' he growled and, retreating into his office, slammed the door savagely behind him.

Fern studied the closed door. That was probably the last she would see of Piers today. She'd formed the habit of sharing Carrie's high tea each evening to avoid having dinner alone with Piers. She could hardly bear to be in the same house as him any more, let alone in the same room. Fortunately he seemed to have a similar aversion to her company, and never deliberately sought her out. Breakfast was the only meal they shared, and, conscious of Carrie's presence, they treated each other with cool civility.

Piers had never referred to their conversation while she'd been in hospital, nor made any attempt to dissuade her from leaving Avonbrook. Doubtless, Fern realised, he was as anxiously counting the days until she left as she was herself.

Yet despite her efforts to distance herself from him physically, Piers was constantly in her mind, the image of his dark, mocking face tormenting her dreams. Sometimes she'd wake to find tears pouring down her cheeks, her whole being numb with desolation and aching loss. Once she'd been woken by the sound of her own voice, shouting out Piers' name. She'd heard the sound of footsteps coming along the landing and pausing outside her door. Hardly daring to breathe, she'd lain rigid, ignoring the gentle tap at the door, sighing with relief as she heard the footsteps receding back along the landing. She seemed to be in a perpetual state of confusion. All she now felt for Piers was burning anger and bitterness. So why did her subconscious mind persist in yearning for him?

Fern bent down and picked up the white envelope from the doormat and stared bleakly at the familiar handwriting. So it had finally arrived. It was almost a relief after all these weeks of waiting. She had been anticipating a letter from a solicitor's, though, hadn't expected Piers to write to her directly to inform her that he had instigated the divorce proceedings. She bit her lip. She knew exactly what was going to be in that letter, so why was she so reluctant to open it?

'I'm going to be late for school,' Carrie wailed plaintively from behind her, hopping agitatedly from one foot to another.

Pushing the unopened letter into the deep pocket of her

navy jacket, Fern slung her handbag over her shoulder, picked up the car keys from the hall table and ushered Carrie out of the cottage.

She dropped Carrie off at school and then retraced her route back to the cottage and then on up the lane to Crofters.

''Morning, David,' she called out as she entered the outer office. She could see him sitting at his desk through the connecting door. He lifted his head, gave a brief smile and bent his head back over the papers in front of him.

'I don't think you'll find that anything's changed,' David had told her on the morning, six weeks ago, when she'd apprehensively arrived at the estate office to resume her old job. But something had changed, Fern soon discovered. The office routine might not have altered, but her working relationship with David was far better than it had been in the past. He seemed less pedantic, less fussy, more considerate. Or perhaps it was simply that, now there was no personal involvement between them, she was less critical and found it easier to relax in his company. David delegated more than he had used to, and Fern welcomed the increased workload that gave her little time to think about anything but the matter in hand during office hours.

Her social life was non-existent. During the long, dark evenings, once Carrie was in bed, she had started to decorate the cottage, often working late into the night until she was physically exhausted. Even then she couldn't always sleep.

Sometimes, she would guiltily remind herself that she had promised to invite Mrs Roberts over for tea one Saturday afternoon, but had so far postponed issuing an invitation. It was inevitable that Piers' name would crop up in any conversation with Mrs Roberts, and Fern knew that she wasn't ready to talk about him with equanimity. She wondered if she would ever be able to mention his name dispassionately.

'I'm going down to the Five Stars for lunch,' David told her as he emerged from his office at one o'clock. 'Fancy coming?'

'Not today, thanks,' Fern smiled. She had accompanied him on occasions, but it was a relaxed, informal arrangement, David never seeming to mind whether she accepted or refused his casual invitations.

Fern replaced the dust cover of her typewriter and stretched her arms above her head. She stood up, slipped on her jacket and stepped outside. The grey, overcast sky suited her mood as she walked briskly down to the river, following the path that wound under the trees to the Ladies' Pool, the autumn leaves lifeless and sodden beneath her feet.

She came into the clearing and gazed down into the water, today as murky and as inhospitable as the overhead sky. The girl who had recklessly dived into the river one hot summer's afternoon seemed as remote as a half-forgotten dream.

Fern raised her left hand in front of her and stared at it for a long moment, and then slowly removed the gold band from her finger. Dry-eyed, she tossed it into the water and watched it disappear into the blackness. So that was that. The end of her marriage. The actual divorce was little more than a formality now.

She reached into her jacket pocket and pulled out the crumpled white envelope. Stony-faced, she tore it open, her eyes widening with incredulity as she extracted the printed card inviting her to attend the evening preview of Piers Warrender's London photographic exhibition. It was such an anticlimax after what she had been expecting that Fern started to laugh, relieving the pent-up tension inside of her. Then her face sobered. Why had Piers sent her this invitation? It simply didn't make sense. She had been aware of the forthcoming exhibition, had read an article about it in a newspaper. There had also been a photograph of an exceptionally grim-faced Piers. But it had never occurred to her that Piers would invite her.

Slowly, she turned the card over in her hand, tensing as she saw Piers' distinctive script on the back, curtly informing her that a car would arrive to collect her at five-thirty on Thursday evening.

The sheer and utter arrogance of the man! Did he think he could just walk back into her life like this? That he only had to crook his little finger and she would come running? Well, she wasn't going to his precious exhibition and that was flat. She couldn't begin to understand what had possessed him to even think that she would.

Determinedly she began walking back towards the estate office. Grateful that David hadn't yet returned from lunch, she perched on her desk, picked up the telephone and dialled the familiar number.

'Mrs Roberts? It's Fern.' So Mrs Roberts had overcome her aversion to answering the telephone, Fern thought, refusing to admit quite how nervous she felt.

'Oh, it's lovely to hear you. How are you? It's not been the same without you, and——'

'I'm fine,' Fern cut through, trying not to appear too bruque and rude. 'Is Piers there?'

'No, my love. He's in London. Sorting out everything for the exhibition. Me and Bert are going up on Friday. Piers is sending a chauffeur-driven car to collect us. Just like we were famous.'

Fern couldn't help smiling at the obvious delight in the older woman's voice.

'He said you'd probably be phoning,' Mrs Roberts continued.

Fern stiffened. 'Oh, really?' How very perceptive of him, she thought acidly.

'Mmm,' Mrs Roberts agreed comfortably. 'And it's all taken care of. Bert and I'll pick up Carrie from school on Thursday and she can stay the night with us. So there's no need to worry on that account.'

'Piers seems to have thought of everything.'

Her sarcasm was lost on the housekeeper, who merely murmured that Piers had always been thoughtful, a remark that made Fern want to scream.

'Well, it's very kind of you, Mrs Roberts,' Fern said firmly, 'but I'm afraid——'

'It's no trouble,' Mrs Roberts cut in blithely, deliberately misunderstanding. 'It'll be lovely to see Carrie again, bless her little heart.'

'But——'

'Goodbye, love. Enjoy yourself.'

Fern stared at the receiver as she heard the click of the telephone being replaced at the other end of the wire. Well, she had certainly tried, she told herself defiantly. But it would appear that matters had been firmly taken out of her hands. She ought to be furious at Piers' high-handedness, making arrangements for Carrie without consulting her, but she felt too weak to feel that strength of emotion. Her legs were wobbly, she registered, and her hands were trembling. She ought to call Mrs Roberts back straight away . . . but she didn't have the heart to disappoint her. The misguided woman obviously believed that there was some sort of reconciliation in the offing.

Who was she trying to fool? She wanted to go to the exhibition, every particle of her being aching to see Piers again. She still loved him, she admitted defeatedly. Had never stopped loving him. The anguish of losing the baby, the only part of Piers that would have ever belonged to her, had made her irrational. She'd become almost crazy with grief, bottling it all up inside her. Convincing herself that she hated Piers, that he was responsible for the miscarriage, had been a way of trying to anaesthetise the pain. It had been less torturing to hate than to love.

She looked down at her bare left hand and her stomach muscles contracted. The tears began to well up in her eyes and, hearing the sound of David's footsteps, she fled to the cloakroom.

The doorbell rang as Fern was putting the finishing touches to her make-up, and she glanced at the alarm clock on her bedside table. The driver was early. Swiftly she checked her appearance in the mirror. Self-esteem demanded that she look her best tonight.

David had been amenable to her taking the afternoon off work and she had rushed out to buy a new dress, finally electing for a figure-hugging gown in midnight-blue with a tantalising V-neck. Freshly washed hair cascaded down her back in gleaming, rich brown waves. Her eyes looked huge under her dark lashes, her skin was clear and pale. Too pale, she judged critically, but she was reluctant to apply too much blusher. She slipped her feet into her evening shoes and hurried downstairs to open the door.

'Piers!' The unexpected sight of the lean, dark-suited figure made her feel weak. 'I didn't realise . . . shouldn't you be in London . . .?' She couldn't think straight, couldn't speak coherently as she gazed at him hungrily. I love you, I love you. The words raged in her head. Desperately she fought for composure, terrified that her eyes would betray her, if they hadn't already done so. He should have told her he would be collecting her himself, should have warned her so that she would have been mentally prepared.

Why didn't he say something? He hadn't moved, was just gazing down at her with dark blue, shadowed eyes.

'I'll fetch my coat,' she said unsteadily, starting to turn away.

'Oh, God, I've missed you!' Dazedly, Fern felt herself being crushed against him, could hear the pounding of his heart, or was it hers? Then she was conscious of nothing but the warmth of his mouth as he kissed her with a fierce, hungry passion that left her breathless and trembling. 'I've been in hell without you,' he muttered hoarsely, covering her face with burning kisses. His arms tightened around her. 'I love you, Fern.'

'No!' The denial was wrenched from her lips. Frantically she struggled to release herself from his imprisoning hold. This was a sick, malicious joke! How could he be so impossibly cruel?

His hand moved to her wrist, his fingers biting into her skin so that she gasped with shock. 'You're hurting me,' she protested.

'You're not running away from me this time,' he answered forcefully, guiding her into the living-room. 'Sit down.'

Weakly, she slumped down on to the sofa.

'Now look at me,' he commanded, sitting down beside her, but making no move to touch her.

Unwillingly, her eyes were drawn to his tense face.

'I love you,' he repeated quietly. 'I think I've loved you from the moment I saw you. Down by the river.' He gave a gentle smile. 'Remember?' he asked softly.

How could she ever forget?

'When you told me you were engaged to David, I felt as if I had been kicked in the stomach,' he continued, his eyes never moving from her face. 'I'd come back to make my peace with him—I never had any intention of claiming the estate—and instead I found I was jealous of him because he had what I wanted more than anything in the world. You.'

Fern's mouth tightened. He made her sound like an object, something to be owned and possessed.

'When we made love the first time, I felt so sure that you felt something for me too. I couldn't believe you could have given yourself to me so completely if you hadn't cared about me.'

He couldn't believe that she'd been so easy, so compliant, so willing, Fern remembered bitterly.

'And afterwards,' he continued softly, 'I wanted to hold you in my arms, tell you how much I loved you.' His mouth twisted. 'Instead I found myself being practically thrown out of your home as if I had the plague.' He paused. 'I thought I'd lost you for good then.'

Fern averted her eyes. She didn't want to hear any more of this. The only reason Piers had ever wanted her in the first place had been because she'd been engaged to David. She'd been a challenge. It was all so obvious now.

'When you agreed to come and work for me, I felt as if I'd been given a second chance. I was determined to take everything slowly this time. A proper old-fashioned courtship.' He smiled ruefully. 'What I hadn't bargained for was the strain I'd find it being in such proximity to you each day and not being able to go near you, not being able to touch you.'

'And that was why you were so damn unpleasant and moody? Because you were frustrated?' Fern enquired sarcastically. She didn't give him time to answer. 'And how exactly did Sally fit into this little scenario?'

His mouth tightened. 'I've already told you. There is, and never has been anything between Sally and me. I've known her all my life. She's like a kid sister.'

Did he seriously expect her to believe that little euphemism? Next he'd be telling her that Sally loved him like a brother, or that they were just good friends.

'So why did you ask Sally to choose the furnishings at Avonbrook?' she asked sweetly.

'Because I didn't have the time or the inclination to do it myself. Before Sally started the owl sanctuary, she was an interior designer.' He saw the startled expression on her face and continued, 'You never had any cause to be jealous of Sally.'

Fern's head shot up. 'I was never——' She stopped in mid-flow, her face flooding with colour.

'So I was right!' Piers exclaimed triumphantly. 'I had my suspicions all along. It was the one thing that gave me hope that you weren't quite as indifferent to me as you appeared to be.'

Fern swallowed. 'Are you trying to tell me that you didn't want to marry me just because of the baby but because you . . . loved me?'

'Yes,' he answered simply and the expression in his eyes made her head spin.

'Why didn't you ask me to stay at Avonbrook then? Why did you let me leave?'

'Because I was hurt and angry. Because I was too proud,' he told her quietly. 'Perhaps I couldn't face being rejected again.'

'So why are you telling me all this now?' Why hadn't he told her weeks ago if it were true that he loved her.

He was silent for a moment before he spoke. 'I hadn't planned to say anything tonight. But when you opened the door to me I saw something in your eyes . . .' He reached out and took hold of her hands. 'You do care for me a little, don't you?' he asked softly.

'I . . .' she choked. She couldn't deny it, not and look into those compelling blue eyes. But neither could she tell him just how much she loved him.

'Will you come back to Avonbrook? Be my wife?'

'No!' She pulled her hands away, her eyes dilating with panic.

'Darling, I know what you've been through,' Piers said soothingly. 'But it'll be different this time, I promise you. I know I can make you happy if only you'll let me.'

She looked at him with glazed eyes. It'll be different this time . . . different this time . . . On how many occasions had Steven said those same words to her? Each time she'd discovered he was having an affair and threatened to leave he'd told her he loved her, that the other woman had meant nothing . . . that it'd be different this time.

'Fern, what's the matter?' Piers' eyes narrowed as they searched her face and then he groaned. 'You don't believe a word I've said, do you?'

Fern licked her dry lips. 'Steven . . . my husband.' My first husband, she thought with sudden hysteria. 'He used to tell me he loved me—every time he'd been unfaithful.' She saw the shock and growing compassion and understanding in Piers' eyes, but continued quickly before he could interrupt. 'I used to think that there was something wrong with me. That I was inadequate, that I'd failed him in some way.' She gulped air into her lungs. 'But now I realise that Steven was incapable of being faithful to any one woman. He saw every woman as a challenge. He didn't want me—until I tried to leave him, and then I suppose I became a challenge again.' She couldn't tell him about that final betrayal with Katherine.

'You think I only want you now because you left me? That I regard you as a challenge?' Piers demanded harshly. 'I'm not Steven,' he rasped.

'No,' Fern agreed shakily, sensing how angry he was. It was impossible to compare the deep, all consuming love she felt for Piers to the brief, immature infatuation she'd once felt for Steven. But didn't Piers understand that that was why she was so terrified? If she put her trust in him, and he betrayed that trust, she didn't think she would have the strength to endure it.

'Your exhibition,' she muttered. 'You'll be late.'

'Damn the exhibition,' he exploded, leaping to his feet and beginning to pace the room.

'It's important,' she reminded him quietly.

'Nothing is important except you.'

'Piers . . . please,' she protested weakly.

He stopped in front of her, gazing down at her. A muscle flickered in his jaw. 'Will you still come to the exhibition with me?' He saw her hesitate. 'Surely you could at least do that for me,' he said bitterly.

She nodded, biting her lip, the temptation to be with him for just a few more hours too great to be ignored any longer. She rose to her feet slowly.

'Where's your wedding ring?' he suddenly asked quietly.

She stiffened, feeling a childish urge to hide her hand behind her back. 'I've mislaid it,' she muttered, lowering her eyes.

'I see,' he said bleakly.

It was dark as Piers drove into central London, the journey there having seemed never ending to Fern. They had exchanged the barest minimum of words, each occupied with their own thoughts.

'Where the hell have you been?' A middle-aged man pounced on Piers agitatedly as they entered the modern, glass-fronted gallery. 'Everyone's here.'

Piers offered no apology or explanation for his late arrival. 'Fern, Arnold James.'

There was a gleam of recognition in Arnold James' eyes that puzzled Fern as she shook his outstretched hand. Then she decided that she must have imagined it as he immediately turned his attention back to Piers. 'Mark Saunders wants to talk to you.'

Fern had never heard the name before, but judging from the deference in Arnold James' voice she guessed that Mark Saunders must be someone important. Perhaps he was a critic, she mused.

A look of resignation crossed Piers' face. 'Arnold?'

'Yes, of course,' the other man smiled. 'I'll be delighted to show Fern round.'

'I won't be long,' Piers murmured quietly and strode away to join a grey-haired, distinguished-looking man, soon becoming engrossed in deep conversation.

'Thank you,' Fern smiled brightly as she accepted a glass of champagne from Arnold. She gazed around the crowded room, watching the expression on people's faces as they moved from one dramatic, stunning photograph to another. The gallery was closed to the general public tonight. These people would be reporters, critics, friends of Piers'.

Some of the photographs were frankly distressing, shocking, graphically illustrating the horrific effects of river and sea pollution on marine life. Vividly, Fern recalled Piers warning her about this aspect of his work. There was one particular photograph of a sea otter vainly trying to clean crude oil from its fur that brought tears to her eyes. She dashed them away furiously. Crying wouldn't help. It was

Piers who was doing something constructive, making people aware of the appalling consequences of man's greed and thoughtlessness on the environment.

She moved on and paused in front of a photograph of nesting eagles.

'Piers spent twelve hours a day for nearly three months sitting in a small hide watching those,' Arnold informed her quietly.

Fern had soon discovered that Arnold owned the gallery and had known Piers for a number of years.

'I was sorry to miss your wedding,' he murmured to her at one point. 'But I was abroad at the time.'

She smiled back at him, not quite certain how to answer that. She was becoming more and more conscious of the number of sideways glances she was attracting from the people around her. It must be because she was with Arnold, she decided, or perhaps people were curious because they had witnessed her arrival with Piers.

Arnold guided her up a shallow flight of wooden steps to the top gallery and Fern looked around her with surprise.

'I didn't realise Piers did fashion photography as well.' She immediately regretted displaying her ignorance as Arnold gave her a puzzled glance, obviously taken aback to discover how little she knew about the man who was supposedly her husband.

'He only undertakes fashion work occasionally now.'

Fern surveyed the beautiful, glamorous women portrayed in front of her, whose faces had adorned the covers of glossy magazines all over the world. How well had Piers known these women? She tried to ignore those icy fingers that curled around her heart, despising herself for that surge of jealousy.

There was a large crowd gathered to the left of her and Fern gazed over their heads to see what was absorbing their attention and froze. The colour drained from her face as she glimpsed the photograph of a slim girl in a pair of faded denim jeans, a wistful expression in her smoky grey eyes, the barest suspicion of a smile hovering on her lips.

When had Piers taken that photograph of her? Fern wondered frantically. How could he have deliberately humiliated her like this, placing that casual photograph of her with windswept hair, clad in that scruffy pair of jeans and old T-shirt, among the ones of these sophisticated, elegant women?

Arnold glanced at her white, shocked face. 'You didn't know about your photograph?'

'No,' she croaked through parched lips.

'I must admit I was a little surprised myself when Piers insisted on including it in his collection, even though it is one of his best.'

Fern hung her head. No wonder Arnold had been amazed. The photograph might be technically brilliant, but the subject matter left a great deal to be desired.

'Piers usually shuns any intrusion into his private life,' Arnold murmured and then smiled. 'You do realise that this is the first time I've ever managed to persuade him to attend one of his own exhibitions in person?'

Fern didn't answer. She didn't know anything about Piers. She never had and she never would. He had tricked her into coming here tonight, had lied about his feelings for her, had mortified her in front of all these people. But why, she wondered despairingly, should he want to be so cruel?

'He must love you very much,' the man by her side murmured softly.

Fern's head jerked up, her eyes returning to the photograph. For the first time she read the simple legend underneath. 'My Wife'. No wonder everyone kept glancing at her, they knew . . . knew she was Piers' wife. The blood raced to her head, setting her face on fire. Piers wanted them to know she was his wife. Because he was proud of her, because in his eyes she was as beautiful and as desirable as any of those other women he had photographed. Because he loved her. That photograph was virtually a public declaration of that love.

'Are you all right?' Arnold asked her anxiously.

'I'm just a bit hot,' she said lamely. 'If I could sit down somewhere cool for a moment . . .' She desperately wanted to be on her own, to try and sort out those erratic thoughts spinning around in her head.

'Come with me.' Arnold led her into an office, sat her down in an armchair and handed her a glass of mineral water.

Fern took a sip from the glass. 'I'm sure you must have people you want to talk to,' she murmured as he hovered over her. 'I'm all right. Really.' She gave him a reassuring smile as he reluctantly moved to the door.

The moment he had departed, Fern sprang to her feet. There was too much energy coursing through her to sit still any longer. Piers loved her! She wanted to shout out the words at the top of her voice, couldn't help that idiotic smile spreading across her face. Abruptly the happiness and elation evaporated. Would Piers ever forgive her for doubting him? She pressed her hand to her mouth, her eyes dark with anguish. How deeply she must have hurt him when she'd rejected him after losing their baby. His need for comfort then must have been as great as hers. And she had failed him!

She spun round as she heard the soft footsteps behind her.

'Arnold told me you weren't feeling well.' Piers' eyes were

cloudy with concern.

'I'm fine.' As she gazed up at Piers, Fern's heart constricted with love. She would trust this man with her life. If only he still wanted her . . .

'Fern?' There was an expression of incredulity on Piers' face as he looked into the grey eyes that were awash with love for him. He put his hands on her shoulders. 'Say it,' he muttered urgently, searching her face intently.

'I l-love you,' she croaked.

With a muffled groan, he drew her into his arms, locking his mouth on hers. Reluctantly he raised his head, and looked down at her. 'You really love me?'

'More than anything in the world,' Fern said simply.

He sat down in the armchair Fern had earlier occupied, and pulled her on to his lap. Tenderly, she ran a finger over the craggy contours of his face. She had never known it was possible to feel so happy.

'I knew the moment I laid eyes on you that you were going to be trouble,' she teased him gently, kissing him on the lips. She frowned. 'Why did your father make that strange will?'

His arms tightened around her. 'Who knows?' he said quietly. 'I never understood my father.'

'You don't still hate David, do you?' she asked a little anxiously.

He kissed the tip of her nose. 'How could I possibly feel anything but gratitude towards him? If it hadn't been for him, I might never have met you.' His eyes gleamed. 'And never found the only secretary who won't walk out on me!'

'Don't you believe it!' Fern grinned.

'On second thoughts,' he murmured, 'I don't think it would be a good idea to reinstate you as my secretary.'

'Why not?' she enquired innocently.

'Because, my dearest wife, I have this awful tendency to become completely distracted when you're around.' He bent his head to demonstrate exactly what form that distraction took.

Neither Fern nor Piers heard the office door open and close again.

A slightly embarrassed-looking Arnold James surveyed the expectant faces turned towards him, and cleared his throat. 'Mr Warrender will be joining us again shortly to answer your questions. He's—er—a little occupied just at present.'

PENNY JORDAN

Sins and infidelities...
Dreams and obsessions...
Shattering secrets
unfold in...

THE HIDDEN YEARS

SAGE — stunning, sensual and vibrant, she spent a lifetime distancing herself from a past too painful to confront... the mother who seemed to hold her at bay, the father who resented her and the heartache of unfulfilled love. To the world, Sage was independent and invulnerable— but it was a mask she cultivated to hide a desperation she herself couldn't quite understand... until an unforeseen turn of events drew her into the discovery of the hidden years, finally allowing Sage to open her heart to a passion denied for so long.

The Hidden Years—a compelling novel of truth and passion that will unlock the heart and soul of every woman.

AVAILABLE IN OCTOBER!
Watch for your opportunity to complete your Penny Jordan set.
POWER PLAY and SILVER will also be available in October.

HARLEQUIN
Romance®

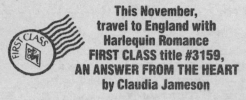

**This November,
travel to England with
Harlequin Romance
FIRST CLASS title #3159,
AN ANSWER FROM THE HEART
by Claudia Jameson**

It was unsettling enough that the company she worked for was being taken over, but Maxine was appalled at the prospect of having Kurt Raynor as her new boss. She was quite content with things the way they were, even if the arrogant, dynamic Mr. Raynor had other ideas and was expecting her to be there whenever he whistled. However Maxine wasn't about to hand in her notice yet; Kurt had offered her a challenge and she was going to rise to it—after all, he wasn't asking her to change her whole life . . . was he?

HARLEQUIN
Romance

A Christmas tradition . . .

Imagine spending Christmas in New
Orleans with a blind stranger and his aged
guide dog—when you're supposed to be
there on your honeymoon!
#3163 Every Kind of Heaven
by Bethany Campbell

Imagine spending Christmas with a man
you once ''married''—in a mock ceremony
at the age of eight!
#3166 The Forgetful Bride
by Debbie Macomber

*Available in December 1991, wherever
Harlequin books are sold.*

RXM